KT-474-222

CP
BJ

Please return / renew by date shown.
ı can renew it at:

AWAKENED
BY HIS TOUCH

AWAKENED BY HIS TOUCH

BY

NIKKI LOGAN

First published in Great Britain 2014
by Mills & Boon, an imprint of Harlequin (UK) Limited.
Large Print edition 2014
Eton House, 18-24 Paradise Road,
Richmond, Surrey, TW9 1SR

© 2014 Nikki Logan

ISBN: 978 0 263 24078 8

Harlequin (UK) Limited's policy is to use papers that
are natural, renewable and recyclable products and made
from wood grown in sustainable forests. The logging
and manufacturing processes conform to the legal
environmental regulations of the country of origin.

Printed and bound in Great Britain
by CPI Antony Rowe, Chippenham, Wiltshire

For Jackie—
protector of all creatures great and small.
(No bees were harmed during the making
of this book)

CHAPTER ONE

ELLIOTT GARVEY LEANED on the bleached timber boardwalk like a seasoned stalker, watching the woman frolicking with her dog where the coastal rock slid down into the aquamarine ocean.

It didn't matter that this lookout and the long, sandy path leading to it were public, the map in his hands and the occasional sign wired to the fence lining the gravel track in this remote, picturesque spot reminded him very clearly that the property all around him was upper-case P private. So, technically, was the beach below. In fact, it barely qualified as a beach since—private or not—it was only about twenty metres long. More a cove, really, eroded out of the hard rock either side of it, protected and quiet.

Back home they'd have turned this into a boat-launching area, for sure. It was perfect for it.

Then again, back home they wouldn't have had anything even remotely like this. Where he was from, further north up the coast, the ruling landform was sand, not the stunning limestone rock forms of the Morgan property. The lookout under his feet 'looked out' over the cove about twenty metres away, as it happened, but its intended view was the spectacular Australian coastline beyond it. Rugged and raw and beaten to death by pounding seas in the off season.

But today the sea was flat and gentle.

His eyes dropped again.

Judging by the very determined way the woman was *not* looking up at him, she was either trying very hard to pretend he wasn't there, spoiling her serenity, or she wasn't supposed to be there. A tourist, maybe? That would explain the long cotton dress that she'd hiked up her bare legs instead of the swimsuit a local would have turned up in. And clearly this was a tourist who liked to travel with her dog. The soggy golden retriever bounded around her, barking and celebrating life in a shower of droplets, and the size of the lead bundled in the woman's right hand suggested her dog was a handful most of the time. But right now it just circled her excitedly as she danced.

Danced? More flowed, really. She practically ebbed in time with the soft waves washing onto the beach and retreating again, her feet lightly skipping in the wet sand. The wet bottom of her long summer dress wanted to cling to her legs, but she kept it hiked up, out of the way, as she splashed in and out of the water with her movements. Dipping and twisting and undulating her whole body to music he couldn't hear.

Out of nowhere, a memory surged into his crowded mind. Of him and his mother, the only trip they'd ever taken away from the city when he was about eight. He'd hung his lean little body half out of the open window of the car she'd borrowed from a friend, overwhelmed to be doing something as exciting as leaving the city, hand-surfing on the wind that whipped past. Riding the current, rising and dipping on it with both hands. Dreaming of the places it would take him if only he were light enough to catch its updraft.

Just as that woman was dancing. There was no wind to speak of down below in the protected little cove, but that didn't seem to cause her the slightest trouble as she moved on air currents no one else could feel. Not him. Not the still coastal wildflowers lining the tiny sandy strip. Not the barely interrupted surface of the water.

Just her, her dog and whatever the heck drugs she must be on to put her in such a sublimely happy place.

Elliott used his camera lens to get a surreptitious

look at her while pretending to photograph the bigger view. Her long hair was as wet and stringy as the golden retriever's, and not all that different in colour, and the water from it soaked anywhere it touched: the fabric of her strappy dress where it criss-crossed her breasts like a bikini top, the golden stretch of her bare shoulders, her collarbones. It whipped and snapped as she circled in the retreating water, her head tipped back to worship the sun, staring right up into it for a moment.

He adjusted the lens just slightly.

The paleness of her skin and the liberal dusting of freckles across it fitted perfectly with the strawberry blonde hair. Maybe if she did this less often out in the harsh Western Australian sun she'd have fewer marks on her skin. But then, maybe if she did this less often she wouldn't have that smile on her face, either. Blazing and almost too wide for the pointed shape of her jaw.

He lowered the lens and stepped back, conscious, suddenly, of his intrusion into her private moment. As he did so, the weathered timber under his left foot creaked audibly and the retriever's sharp ears didn't miss it. Its sandy snout pointed up in his direction immediately, joyous barking suspended, and it crossed straight to the woman's side. She stopped and bent to place her free hand reassuringly on the dog's shoulder but—luckily for Elliott—she didn't follow the direction of its intent stare.

Not waiting to be busted, he retreated down the lookout steps and along the path to the gravel track where his luxury car waited. The only car here, he suddenly realised.

Ah, well, if Little Miss Lives-Life-on-the-Edge liked to take that skin outside at noon, trespass on private property and stare directly into the sun, then she was probably illegally camped around here somewhere, too.

Either way...? Officially none of his business. He was here to talk the Morgans into taking their company global. Not to police their perimeter security for them.

He had one more shot at this. One more chance to eclipse bloody Tony Newton and his questionable success and get the vacant partnership. Being good—or even great—at your job was no longer enough. He needed to be *astounding* at what he did in order to win his spot on the partners' board and cement his future. And Morgan's was the brand to do it. Newton was too busy schmoozing his cashed-up tech and dot-com clients to notice what was right under all their noses—that Morgan's was about so much more than honey. Whether the board realised it or not.

And if they didn't…?

That was okay. That was what they had him for.

'What is a "realiser" exactly, Mr Garvey?' Ellen Morgan asked him politely an hour later, studying his slick business card.

Falling straight into his corporate patter was second nature. 'Realisers are charged with the responsibility of identifying clients with potential and then helping them *realise* that potential.'

'That's a strange sort of job, I'd have thought,' announced Robert Morgan as he marched into the living room with two cups of coffee to match the one his wife already cradled and handed one to Elliott.

'It's a speciality role. A different focus to my colleagues'.'

Ellen didn't quite bristle, but offence tickled at the edges of her words. 'You believe we have unrealised potential here, Mr Garvey? We consider ourselves quite innovative for our industry.'

'Please, call me Elliott,' he repeated, despite knowing it was probably pointless. He wasn't in with them yet. 'You absolutely *are* innovative. You dominate the local market and you're top three nationally—' if they weren't a company like Ashmore Coolidge wouldn't touch them '—and yet there's always room for growth.'

And profit. And acclaim. Particularly acclaim.

'We're honey farmers, Mr Garvey. One of a multitude in the international marketplace. I'm not sure there's room for us overseas.'

As if that was all they were, and as if their operations weren't perched on one of the most stunning and sought-after peninsulas on Western Australia's ten-thousand-kilometre coastline.

But it wasn't the local market that interested him. 'My job is to help you make room.'

'By nudging someone else out?' Ellen frowned.

'By being competitive. And ethical. And visible.' Currently they were only a twofer.

'You think the enormous sun on our packaging fails to stand out on the shelf?'

The new voice was soft, probing, and very much rhetorical... And coming from the doorway.

Elliott turned as Helena Morgan walked into the room. Ellen and Robert's daughter and reputedly the talent behind Morgan's ten-year surge to the top—

His eyes dropped to the sandy, damp golden retriever that galloped in behind her.

—and also the woman from the beach.

Of course she was.

All the rapport he'd built with the parents since arriving suddenly trembled on whether or not Helena Morgan realised he was the one who had been watching her with her wet dress clinging to her body earlier.

If she did he was dead in the water.

But she didn't comment, and she didn't even glance at him as she crossed into the kitchen, trailing elegant fingertips along the benchtop until she reached the extra coffee mug Robert Morgan had left out. For her, presumably. As tactics went, her dismissal was pretty effective.

'I'm not talking about shelf presence,' Elliott said in his best boardroom voice, eager to take back some control. 'I'm talking about market presence.'

'Wilbur!' Ellen Morgan scolded the dog, who had shoved his soggy face between her and her coffee for a pat. He wagged an unremorseful tail. 'Honestly, Laney...'

The woman made a noise halfway between a whistle and a squeak and the dog abandoned its efforts for affection and shot around the sofa and into the kitchen to stand respectfully beside Helena.

Laney.

The nickname suited her. Still feminine, but somehow...earthier.

'Our customers know exactly where to find us,' Laney defended from the kitchen.

'Do new ones?'

She paused—the reboiled kettle in one hand and two fingers of the other hooked over her coffee cup edge—and looked towards him. 'You don't think we do well enough on the ones we have?'

One Morgan parent watched her; the other watched him. And he suddenly got the feeling he was being tested. As if everything hinged on how he managed this interaction.

'All markets change eventually,' he risked.

'And we'll change with it.'

She poured without taking her eyes off him, and his chest tightened just a hint as steam from the boiling water shimmied up past her vulnerable fingers. That was a fast track to the emergency room. But it certainly got his attention.

As it was supposed to.

'But we've never been greedy, Mr Garvey. I see no reason to start being so now.'

Her use of his name gave him the opening he needed as she walked back into the living room with her fresh coffee. 'You have the advantage of me.'

Half challenge, half criticism. And formal, but not out of place; she had a very…*regal*…air about her. The deliberate way she moved. The way she regarded him but didn't quite deign to meet his eyes.

'Apologies, Mr Garvey,' Robert interjected, 'this

is our daughter and head apiarist Helena. Laney, this is Mr Elliott Garvey of Ashmore Coolidge.'

She stretched her free hand forward, but not far enough for him to reach easily. Making him come to her. Definite princess move. Then again, the Morgans did hold all the power here. For now. It was a shame he had no choice but to take the two steps needed to close his hand over her small one. And a shame his curiosity wouldn't let him not. Maybe her skin wasn't as soft as it looked.

Though it turned out it was. His fingers slid over the undulating pads of hers until their palms pressed warmly and his skin fairly pulsed at the contact.

'A financier?' she said, holding his hand longer than was appropriate.

'A realiser,' he defended, uncharacteristically sensitive to the difference all of a sudden.

And then—finally—she made formal eye contact. As if his tone had got him some kind of password access. Because he was taller than her—even with those legs that had seemed to go on for ever down at the beach—her looking up at him from closer quarters lifted her thick lashes and gave him a much better look at deep grey irises surrounded by whites of a clarity he never saw in the city.

Or in the mirror.

Healthy, fresh-air-raised eyes. And really very

beautiful. Yet still not quite…*there*. As if her mind was elsewhere.

Some crazy part of him resented not being worthy of her full attention when this meeting and what might come out of it meant so much to him. Perhaps cautious uninterest was a power mechanism on the Morgan property.

Effective.

'I studied the proposal you emailed,' she said, stepping back and running the hand that had just held his through her dog's wet coat, as if she was wiping him off.

'And?'

'And it was…very interesting.'

'But you aren't very interest*ed*?' he guessed aloud.

Her smile, when it came, changed her face. And instantly she was that girl down by the beach again. Dancing in the surf. The mouth that was a hint too big for her face meant her smile was like the Cheshire Cat's. Broad and intriguing. Totally honest. Yet hiding everything.

'It sounds terrible when you say it like that.'

'Is there another way to say no?'

'Dozens.' She laughed. 'Or don't you hear it very often?'

Her parents exchanged a momentary glance. Not

of concern at their daughter's bluntness, rather more…speculative. She ignored them entirely.

'I'd like to learn more about your new processes,' he risked, appealing to her vanity since their new processes were *her* new processes. 'And perhaps go further into what I have in mind.'

She dismissed it out of hand. 'We don't do tours.'

'You'll barely notice me. I'm particularly good at the chameleon thing—'

Two tiny lines appeared between brows a slightly lighter colour than her still damp hair and he realised that wasn't the way in either.

'And your Ashmore Coolidge health-check is due soon anyway. Two birds, one stone.'

That, *finally*, had an impact. So Laney Morgan was efficient, if nothing else. His firm required biennial business health-checks on their clients to make sure everything was solid. By contract.

'How long? An hour?' she asked.

His snort surprised her.

'A day, at least. Possibly two.'

'We're to put you up on no notice?'

Who knew a pair of tight lips could say so much?

'No. I'll get a room in town…'

'You will not,' Ellen piped up. 'You can have a chalet.'

He and Laney both snapped their faces towards her at the same time.

'Mum...'

'You have accommodation?' That wasn't in their file.

Ellen laughed. 'Nothing flash—just a couple of guest dwellings up in the winter paddock.'

That was the best opening he was going to get. Staying on the property, staying close, was the fastest way to their compliance he could think of. 'If you're sure?'

'Mum!'

Laney's face gave nothing away but her voice was loaded with meaning. Too late. The offer was made. A couple of days might be all he needed to get to know all of the Morgan clan and influence their feelings about taking their operation global.

'Thank you, Ellen, that's very generous.'

Her face gave nothing away, but Helena's displeasure radiated from the more subtle tells in her body—her posture, the acute angle of her neck, as if someone was running fingernails down a chalkboard on some frequency the rest of them couldn't hear. Except her dog couldn't hear it either—he'd flopped down behind the sofa, fast asleep.

'Laney, will you show Elliott up to the end chalet, please?'

That sweet, motherly voice wasn't without its own strength and it brooked no argument.

When Laney straightened she was back to avoiding eye contact again. She smiled with as few muscles as possible, the subtext flashing in neon.

'Sure.'

She made the squeak noise again and her dog leapt to attention. She turned, trailed her hand along the back of the sofa and then around the next one, and reached for the cluster of leather he'd seen in her hand down at the beach from where it now hung over the back of a dining chair. As she bent and fitted it around the crazy, tearaway dog it totally changed demeanour; became attentive and professional. Then she stood and held the handle loosely in her left hand.

And everything fell into place.

The death-defying coffee pour. The standoffish outstretched hand. The lack of hard eye contact.

Laney Morgan wasn't a princess or judgmental— at least she wasn't *only* those things.

Laney Morgan—whom he'd seen dancing so joyously on the beach, who had taken a family honey business and built it into one of the most successful in the country, and who had just served him his own genitals on a plate—couldn't see.

CHAPTER TWO

'YOU'RE BLIND,' ELLIOTT GARVEY murmured from Laney's right, the moment they were outside.

'You're staring.'

'I wasn't,' he defended after a brief pause, his voice saturated with unease.

'I could feel it.' And then, at the subtle catch in his breath. '*Practically* feel it, Mr Garvey. Not literally.' Though he certainly wouldn't be the first to expect her to have some kind of vision-impaired ESP.

He cleared his throat. 'You hide it well.'

Wilbur protested her sudden halt with a huff of doggie breath.

'I don't *hide* it at all.'

'Right, no…sorry. Poor choice of words.'

Confusion pumped from him and she got the sense that he was a man who very rarely let himself get flustered. It was tempting to play him, just a little, but her mother had raised her never to exploit the discomfiture of others. Because if *she* expected to be taken at face value how could she do less for anyone else?

Even intruding corporate types from the city.

She adjusted her trajectory at Wilbur's slight left tug and passed through the first gate beside her dog. 'I've had twenty-five years to perfect things, Mr Garvey. Plus the direction of your breathing gave you away.'

'Elliott.'

Then he fell silent again and she wondered if he was looking around at their farm…or at her still? Scrutiny never had sat lightly on her.

'He's very focussed. Wilbur, was it?'

Okay, neither of the above. He'd managed to zero in on her favourite talking point.

'Captain Furry-Pants to his friends.' She smiled. 'When the harness is on, he's on. When it comes off he's just a regular dog. Making up for lost time by being extra goofy. Getting it out of his system.'

They walked on to the steady reassurance of the sound of gravel crunching under eight feet.

'Your property is beautiful. This peninsula is extraordinary.'

'Thank you.'

'Have you ever lived anywhere else?'

'Why would I? It's perfect here. The wildlife. The space.'

His lagging steps pulled him further behind. 'The beaches…'

There was more than just tension in his voice. There was apology in the way he cleared his throat. She quarter-turned her head back towards him as she continued onward and the penny dropped.

Wilbur's quiet growls down by the water… 'That was you?'

'I was using the lookout. I didn't realise it over-looked a private beach. I'm sorry.'

Had he watched her wading? Dancing? It took a lot to make her feel vulnerable these days. Not that she was going to let him know that.

She tossed her hair back. 'You got a first-hand demonstration of Wilbur in off-harness mode, then.'

His crunching footsteps resumed. 'Yeah, he was having a ball.'

'He loves to swim.'

Awesome—she was like a radio stuck on Channel Wilbur. Time for some effort. 'So you must have drawn the short straw, being sent by your firm so far from the city?'

'Not at all. I chose to come. Morgan's isn't on anyone else's radar.'

That got her attention. 'You make it sound like a competition.'

'It is. It's the best part of the job. Finding raw talent, developing it.'

Realising it. She stepped with Wilbur around an obstacle and then smelled it as she passed. A cowpat. Behind her, Garvey grunted. Presumably, he hadn't been so lucky. She didn't stop and he caught up straight away.

'Did you miss it?'

'Just.'

He didn't sound irked. If anything, that was amusement warming his voice. Her lips twisted. 'Sorry, we have a couple of milk cows that free range.'

Silence reigned for the next minute or two and, again, she had to assume he was looking around at the farm, its outbuildings and condition. Critically? Morgan's had modern facilities to go with its spectacular coastal location but being judged had never sat comfortably on her. The smell of tiny wildflowers kicked up from underfoot.

'So if it's a competitive process, and we're not on anyone else's radar, does that mean no one else at your firm believes we have potential?'

He took his time answering. Something she appreciated. He wasn't a man to rush to fill a silence.

'It means they lack vision. And they're not paying attention.'

Okay, for a city boy he definitely had a great voice. Intelligent and measured and just the right amount of gravel. It was only when she gave him another mental tick that she realised she'd started a list.

'But you are?'

'I've been tracking your progress a long time—' His voice shifted upwards a semi-tone. 'Are those tyres?'

The rapid subject-change threw her, but he had to mean the chalets that they were approaching.

'Dad had one of his recycling frenzies a couple of years ago and made a couple up for family and friends—' *and inconvenient visitors from the city* '—when they visit. Tyres and rammed earth on the outside but pretty flash on the inside. Bed, open fire and privacy.' For them as much as their guests. 'And what I'm reliably informed are some pretty spectacular ocean views.'

Tension eased out of him on a satisfied sigh. 'You're not wrong. One hundred and eighty de-grees.'

She stopped at the door to the chalet on the end, used the doorframe to orientate herself and pointed left. 'Manufacturing is over that way, beach is down that track, and the first of the bee yards is up behind this hill. You should probably take a bit of time to settle in. Can you find your way back to your car for your things?'

Idiot, she chided herself. He could probably see it from here. There was nothing between them and the Morgan's car park but open paddock. What was wrong with her? Maybe her brain cells were drunk on whatever that was coming off him.

'Yep. I'm good. Do I need to be somewhere at a particular time?'

'Are you allergic to bees?'

'Only one way to find out.'

The man faced life head-on. Her favourite direction. 'Well, if you feel like living dangerously, come on up the hill in twenty minutes. I'll be checking the bees.'

Soonest started, soonest done. She turned and thrust the chalet key at him and warm fingers brushed hers as he took it.

'Do I need protective gear?' he murmured.

'Not unless you plan on plunging your hands into the hives. This first community is pretty chill.' Which wasn't true of all their bees, but definitely true of her favourites. 'But maybe wear sunglasses.'

'Okay. Thanks, Laney.'

His voice lifted with him as he stepped up into the unlocked chalet but there was an unidentifiable something else in his tone. Sorrow? Why would he be sad? He was getting his way. She thought about protesting his presumption in using her nickname but then remembered what he'd probably seen down on the beach. Niceties, after that, seemed rather pointless. Although it did still have the rather useful value of contrasting with her own formality.

'You're welcome, *Mr Garvey*.'

With a flick of her wrist Wilbur full-circled and walked her down the hill and back through the gate, leaving the subtle dismissal lingering in the air behind her. As soon as she turned him left, towards one of the closest bee yards, Wilbur realised where they were going and he lengthened his strides, excited. He loved the beach first and the bees second. Because when she was elbow-deep in bees he was free to romp around the yards as much as he wanted.

Laney was always pleasantly breathless when she crested the hill to the A-series hives, and, as she always did, she stalled at the top and turned to survey the property. The landscape of her imagination. It was branded into her brain in a way that didn't need the verification of sight—the layout, the view as it had been described to her over the years. Three generations of buildings where all their manufacturing and processing was done, the endless ocean beyond that.

She had no way of knowing how like the real thing her mixed-sense impression of it was, but ultimately it didn't matter what it really looked like. In her mind it was magnificent. And she had the smells and the sounds and the pristinely fresh air to back it up.

So when Elliott Garvey complimented the Morgan property she knew it was genuine. They'd had enough approaches from city folk wanting to buy in to know that it was one of the better-looking properties in the district. But that was not why her family loved it. At least it wasn't *only* why they loved it. They loved it because it was fertile and well-positioned, in a coastal agricultural district, and undulating and overflowing with wildflowers, and because it backed on two sides onto nature reserves packed with Marri and Jarrah trees which meant their bees had a massive foraging range and their honey had a distinctive geo-flavour that was popular with customers.

And because it was home. The most important of all. Where she'd lived since her parents had first brought her home from the hospital, swaddled in a hand-loomed blanket.

That was the potential they all believed in. Regardless of what else Call-Me-Elliott Garvey saw in Morgan's.

* * *

What was the protocol in this kind of situation? Should he stomp his feet on the thick grassed turf so that she could hear him coming? Cough? Announce himself?

 In the end Wilbur took matters into his own paws and came bounding over, collar tags jangling, alerting Helena to Elliott's presence as effectively as a herald. The dog was mostly dry now, and had traded damp dog smell for fresh grass smell, and he responded immediately to Wilbur's eager-eyed entreaty with a solid wrestle and coat-rub.

'Hey, there, Captain Furry-Pants.' Well, they were kind of friends now, right? And Wilbur's haunches *were* particularly furry. 'Still got energy left?'

'Boundless,' Laney said without looking around, her attention very much on what she was doing at one of dozens of belly-height boxes.

She'd thrown a long-sleeved shirt over her summer dress but that was it for the protective wear he'd imagined they would wear on a busy apiary. One for the 'risks' column in his report. A handful of bees busied themselves in the air around her but their orbit was relaxed. A steady stream of others took off for the fields behind them and made way for the ones returning.

It was as busy as any of the airports he'd passed through in his time. And there'd been many.

He slid his sunglasses on and felt, again, a pang at Laney's earlier kindness: a woman who had no use of her eyes taking the trouble to watch out for his.

'Can I approach?'

'Sure. Watch your feet in case any bees are on the grass.'

His focus shifted from the airborne bees to the possibility of stealth bees underfoot. There were one or two. 'Are they sick?'

Her laugh caused a whisper of a ripple in the steady hum coming off the bees. Like a tiny living echo. 'They're just resting. Or moisture-seeking.'

'How do you not step on them?'

'I slide rather than tread,' she said, without taking her focus off what she was doing. 'Kind of a roller-blading motion. It gives them a chance to take off.'

He stepped up closer. 'You've rollerbladed?'

'Of course.'

As if it was such a given.

'That's probably close enough,' she confirmed as he moved just behind her shoulder. 'And if I say run, do it. Straight back downhill to the carriage.'

He studied her face for any indication that she was kidding. There was nothing. 'Is that my safety induction?'

'Sure is. It's a fairly simple rule. Don't touch and don't stick around if things get active.'

And leave a blind woman undefended while bees swarmed? Not going to happen. But they could argue that out after they were both safe.

Her fingers dusted over the surface of the open hive, over the thronging mass itself, but the bees didn't seem to mind. Some hunkered down under her touch, others massed onto the back of her hand and crawled off the other side, or just held on for the free ride. None seemed perturbed.

'What are you doing, exactly?' he asked.

'Just checking them.'

'For…?'

'For hive beetle.'

'What's your process?'

He held his most recent breath. Would she hear the subtext clearly? *How can you do that, blind?*

But if she did, she let it go with a gracious smile. Just as well, because he had a feeling that a lot of his questions were going to start that way.

'The bees are kind of…fluid. They move under touch. But the beetles are wedged in hard. A bit like pushing your fingers through barley in search of a pinhead.'

There was a truckload of bees swarming over the hive and Laney's hands, but something about the totally unconcerned way she interacted with them—and her own sketchy safety gear—gave him the confidence to lean in as she pulled a frame out of several racked in the hive. It was thick with bees and honeycomb and—sure enough—the odd tiny black beetle.

Which she cut mercilessly in half with her thumbnail as her fingers found them.

'Pest?'

'Plague.' She shook her head. 'But we have it better here on the peninsula. And want to keep it that way.'

Her bare fingers forked methodically through the thick clumps of bees.

'How are you not a mass of stings?'

'My fingers are my eyes, so I can't work with gloves. Besides, this hive isn't aggressive—they'll only react to immediate threat.'

'And your hands aren't a threat?'

'I guess not.'

Understandable, perhaps. Her long fingers practically caressed them, en masse, each touch a stroke. It was almost seductive.

Or maybe that was just him. He'd always been turned on by competence.

'Hear that note?' She made a sound that was perfectly pitched against the one coming from the bees. 'That's Happy Bee sound.'

'As opposed to…?'

'Angry Bee sound. We're Losing Patience sound. We're Excited sound. They're very expressive.'

'You really love them.'

'I'd hope so. They're my life's work.'

Realising was his life's work, but did he love it? Did his face light up like hers when he talked about his latest conquest? Or did he just value it because he had a talent for it, and he liked being good at things. A lot. Getting from his boss the validation he'd never had as a kid.

Laney gave the bees a farewell puff of smoke from the mini bellows sitting off to one side and then slid the frame back into its housing, her fingertips guiding its way. They spidered across to the middle frame and he grew fixated on their elegant length. Their neat, trim, unvarnished nails.

She lifted another frame. 'This feels heavy. A good yield.'

It was thick with neatly packed honeycomb, waxed over to seal it all in. He mentioned that.

'The frames closest to the centre are often the fullest,' she explained. 'Because they focus their effort around the brood frame, where the Queen and all her young are.'

It occurred to him that he should probably be taking notes—that was what a professional would have been doing. A professional who wasn't being dazzled by a pretty woman, that was.

'Seriously? The most valuable members of the community in one spot, together? That seems like bad planning on their part.'

'It's not like a corporation, where the members of the board aren't allowed to take the same flight.' She laughed. 'There's no safer place than the middle of a heavily fortified hive. Surrounded by your family.'

'In theory…'

In his world, things hadn't operated quite that way.

'If something does happen to the Queen or the young they just work double-time making a new queen or repopulating. Colonies bounce back quickly.'

Not all that different from Ashmore Coolidge. As critical as their senior staff were, if someone defected the company recovered very quickly and all sign of that person sank without a trace. A fact all the staff were graphically reminded of from time to time to keep them in line.

'So the bees work themselves to death, supporting the royal family?'

'Supporting *their* family. They're all of royal descent.' She clicked the frame back into position. 'Isn't that what we all do, ultimately? Even humans?'

'Not everyone. I support myself.'

She turned and faced him and he felt as pinned as if she could see him. 'Are you rich?'

She wasn't asking to be snoopy, so he couldn't be offended. 'I'm comfortable.'

'Do you keep all the money you make for Ashmore Coolidge?'

No. But she knew that, so he didn't bother answering.

'Your firm gets the bulk of the money you generate for them and that goes to…who? The partners?'

In simple terms. 'They work hard, too.'

'But they already get a salary, right? So they get their own reward for their work, and also most of yours?'

'We have shareholders, too.'

Why the hell was he so defensive around her? And about this. Ashmore Coolidge's corporate structure was the same as every other glass and chrome tower in the city.

'A bunch of strangers who've done *none* of the work?' She held up a hand and dozens of bees skittled over it. 'You're working yourself into the ground supporting other people's families, Mr Garvey. How is that smarter than what these guys do?'

He stared at the busy colony in the hive. Utterly lost for words at the simple truth of her observation.

'Everything they do, they do for the betterment of their own family.' Her murmurs soothed the insects below her fingers. 'And their lives may be short, but they're comfortable. And simply focussed. Every bee has a job, and as long as they fulfil their potential then the hive thrives.' She stopped and turned to him. 'They're *realisers*—just like you.'

Off in the distance Wilbur lurched from side to side on his back in the long grass, enjoying the king of all butt-scratches. Utterly without dignity, but completely happy. As simple as the world she'd just described.

Elliott frowned. He got a lot of validation from being in Ashmore Coolidge's top five. Success in their business was measured in dollars, yet he'd never stopped to consider exactly how that money flowed. Always away from him, even if he got to keep a pretty generous part of it. Which was just a clue as to how much more went to their shareholders. Nameless, faceless rich people.

'I send money to my mother—'

The moment the words were out he wanted to drag them back in, bound and gagged. Could he be any more ridiculous? Laney Morgan wasn't interested in his dysfunctional family.

He was barely interested in it.

A woman with a Waltons family lifestyle would never understand what it had been like growing up with no money, no prospects and no one to tell him it was perfectly okay to crave more. Leaving him feeling ashamed when he did.

But a smile broke across her face, radiant and golden, and a fist clenched somewhere deep in his chest.

'That's a good start. We'll make a bee of you yet.'

He fell to silence and watched Laney beetle-busting. Fast, methodical. Deadly. Inexplicably, he found it utterly arresting.

'I'm sorry,' she murmured eventually.

'For what?'

'For generating that silence. I didn't mean to be dismissive of your work.'

Think fast, Garvey. It's what you're paid for. 'I was thinking about a world in which people only acted for family benefit and whether it could work in real terms.' Better than admitting he was transfixed by her.

'You think not?'

'I question whether that kind of limited focus is sustainable. Outside of an apiary.'

She gave the bees one last puff of smoke and then refitted the lid with her fingers. 'Limited?'

'You've grown Morgan's significantly over the past ten years. Why?'

'To make better use of the winter months. To exploit more of the by-products that were going to waste. To discover more.'

'Yet you're not interested in continuing that growth?'

Time he stopped being hypnotised by this woman and her extraordinary talents and got back in the game, here.

Her sigh said she was aware of it too. 'We don't need to. We're doing really well as is.'

'You're doing really well for a family of four and a smallish staff.' Or so the Morgan's file said. Then again, that same file had totally neglected to mention Laney's blindness.

'That's all we are.'

'So your growth is limited by your ambition. And your ambition—' *or perhaps lack of it* '—is determined by your needs.'

Those long fingers that had done such a fine job of soothing the bees fisted down by her sides. 'Morgan's would never have come to your attention if we lacked ambition, Mr Garvey.'

Elliott. But he wasn't going to ask her again. He wasn't much on begging.

'Yet it is limited. You've expanded as much as you want to.'

'You say that like it's a bad thing. This is our business—surely how hard or otherwise we pursue it is also up to us?'

'But you have so much more potential.'

'Why would we fight for a market share we don't need or want? Surely that's the very definition of sustainable? Not just taking for taking's sake.'

He stared. She was as alien to him as her bees. 'It's not *taking*, Laney, it's *earning.*'

'I earn the good sleep I have every night. I earn the pleasure my job brings to me and to the people we work with. I earn the feeling of the sun on my face and the little surge of endorphins that hearing Happy Bees gives me. I am already quite rewarded enough for my work.'

'But you could have so much more.'

Her shoulders rose and fell a few times in silence. 'You mean I could *be* so much more?'

It was the frostiest she'd been with him since walking into the living room earlier. 'Look, you are extraordinary. What you've achieved in the past decade despite your—'

She lifted one eyebrow.

Crap.

'Disability? It's okay to say it.'

Which meant it absolutely wasn't.

'Despite the *added complexities* of your vision loss,' he amended carefully. 'I can only imagine what you'd be capable of on the world stage with Ashmore Coolidge's resources behind you.'

'I have no interest in being on stage, Mr Garvey. I like my life exactly as it is.'

'That's because you have no experience outside of it.'

'So I lack ambition and now I'm also naïve? Is this how you generally win clients over to your point of view?'

'Okay. I'm getting off track. What I'm asking for is an open mind. Let me discover all the aspects of your business and pitch you some of the ideas I have for its growth. Let's at least hash it out so that we can both say that we've listened.'

'And you think one overnight stay and a tour of our operation is going to achieve that?'

'No, I absolutely don't. This is going to be a work in progress. I'd like to make multiple visits and do some more research in between. I'd like the opportunity to change your mind.'

She shrugged, but a hint of colour flamed up around the collar of her shirt. Had the thought of him returning angered her or—his stomach tightened a hint—had it interested her?

'It's your time to waste.'

'Is that a yes?'

'It's not my decision to make. I'll talk to my parents tonight. We'll let you know tomorrow.'

CHAPTER THREE

WHY WAS IT that everyone thought they knew what she wanted better than she did?

Bad enough fielding her mother's constant thoughts on why she should get out more and meet people and her father's endless determination that not a single opportunity in life be denied her. Only her brother treated her with the loving disdain of someone you'd shared a womb with.

Now even total strangers were offering their heavily loaded opinions.

She'd met Elliott Garvey's type before. Motivated by money. She couldn't quite bring herself to suggest it was *greed*, because she'd seen no evidence of excess on his part, but then again she'd only known him for an hour or two.

Though it definitely felt longer.

Particularly the time out by the hives. She'd been distracted the whole time, feeling his heat reaching out to her, deciding he was standing too close to both her and the hives but then having his voice position proving her wrong. Unless he occupied more space than the average person? Maybe he was a large man?

He hadn't sounded particularly puffed after his hike up the hill. Or while they'd power-walked to the carriage. There was no way of knowing without touching him. Or asking outright.

Excuse me, Mr Garvey, are you overweight?

He'd been just as direct with her, asking about her vision, so maybe he was the kind of man you *could* ask that of? Except she wasn't the kind of woman who could ever ask it. Not without it sounding—and feeling—judgemental. And, as a lifelong recipient of the judgement of others, she was the last person to intentionally do it to another.

Nope. Elliott Garvey was a puzzle she would have to piece together incrementally. Subtly, or her mother would start pressing the paper for wedding invitations. But she couldn't take too long or he'd be gone back to his corporate world, because she felt certain that her father wouldn't agree to a series of visits. He'd only agreed to this one to be compliant with their financial management requirements.

Which didn't mean she wouldn't enjoy the next twenty-four hours. As much as she hated to admit it, he smelled really good. Most men in their district let the surf provide their hygiene and they either wore Eau de Farm or they bathed in fifty-per-cent-off cologne before driving into town to try and pick up. Elliott Garvey just had a tangy hint of…something…coming off him. And he was smart, too, which made his deep tones all the easier to listen to. Nothing worse than a phone sex voice on a man who had nothing of interest to say.

Not that she necessarily agreed with what he had to say, but he was astute and respectful, and he'd been about as tactful questioning her about her sight as anyone she'd ever met. Those first awkward moments notwithstanding.

'So you'd be happy to show him around, Laney?' her father repeated as they laid the table in their timber and glass home for dinner that evening.

Spending a bit more time in Elliott Garvey's company wasn't going to be an excruciating hardship. He was offering her his commercial expertise for free and she'd be happy to see the Morgan's range reflected through the filter of that expertise. Maybe there'd be a quiet thing or two she could implement here on the farm. Without taking them global. There was still plenty of scope for improvement without worrying about world domination.

And then there was the whole enjoying the sound and smell of him…

'Sure.'

She reached over one of the timber chairs and flattened her palm on the table, then placed the fork at her thumb and the knife at her widespread little finger. 'It's only one more day.'

'Actually, I was thinking of agreeing to his request,' her father said.

The chair-leg grunted on the timber floor as she stumbled against it. 'To let him come back again?'

'I'd like to hear the man out.'

'Surely it couldn't take more than a day to give him a courtesy listen?'

'Not if he's to see the full range of our operations first hand. Too much of it is seasonal.'

Spring and summer were all about honey-harvesting, but the remaining six months of the year they concentrated on other areas of their operation. They lived and worked through winter on the back of the honey harvest. Just like the bees did.

'How many times?'

'That's up to him,' her father suggested. 'It's business as usual for us.'

'Easy for you to say—you're not tasked with babysitting.'

'You're the best one to talk turkey with the man, Laney. Most of what we now do are your initiatives.'

'They're *our* initiatives, Dad. The whole family discussed and agreed.'

Well, she'd discussed and her parents had agreed. Owen had just shrugged.

'But you created them.'

'Someone else created them. I just suggested we adopt them.'

'Stop playing down your strengths,' he grumbled. As usual.

'Would you rather I took credit for the work of others?' she battled. As usual.

Frustration oozed from his tone. 'I'd rather you took some credit for yourself from time to time. Who knows? If you impress him enough there might be a job in it for you.'

'I have a job here.'

'A better job.'

The presumption that her job wasn't already about the best occupation a person could hope for really rankled. 'Why would they hire me, Dad? Not a lot of call for apiarists in the city.'

'Why *wouldn't* they hire you? You're as smart and capable as anyone else. More so.'

'How about because I know nothing about their industry?'

'He's trained to recognise raw talent. He'd be crazy not to take you on.'

Laney got the tiniest thrill at the thought of being *taken on* in any way by Elliott Garvey, but she fought it. 'You don't just hire someone because they seem generally capable, Dad.'

'You're as worthy as anyone of your chance.'

Dread pooled thick and low. *Oh, here we go...* 'Dad, promise me you won't do the whole Laney-sell job.'

As he was so very wont to do. Over and over during her childhood, much to her dismay. But the thought of him humiliating her like that with Elliott Garvey... *Ugh.*

'I'll promise no such thing. I'm proud of my daughter and her achievements and not too shy to admit it.'

'He's here to study our operations, not—'

'I liked him,' her mother piped up, apropos of pretty much nothing, as she placed a heavy dish on the table with a punctuating clunk. Chicken stew, from the delicious aroma. All organic, like the rest of their farm. 'He's handsome.'

Her father grunted. 'Don't change the subject, Ellen.'

'You think everyone's handsome, Mum.' Laney lowered her voice instinctively as she and her father helped ferry clean plates to the table, even though she'd heard Elliott Garvey's expensive tyres on the driveway gravel about twenty minutes earlier. 'Besides, what do looks have to do with a person's integrity or goodness?'

'I can't comment on those until I've shared a meal with the man. So can we please just do that before setting our minds in any particular direction?'

'You'll have to invite him first, and he goes home tomorrow afternoon.' So there went the dinner plan. Conveniently.

'I *have* invited him. That's his setting you just laid.'

She straightened immediately. No. She'd only set the table for the usual four. 'Where's Owen?'

'Chasing some surfer tourist,' his father muttered.

At twenty-five she might still be a work in progress, but her twin had pretty much stopped emotional development at eighteen. *Whatever* was Owen's perpetual outlook. If he was around to give one and not off surfing the latest hot break.

'He's taking her for a pizza, Robert. He had his Saturday night shirt on.'

Oh, well…look out, Surfer Girl, then. If her brother had bothered with a clean shirt he was definitely on the make. Girls and surfing were about the only things Owen took seriously.

'And you didn't think to just let us enjoy a quiet dinner without him?' Laney muttered.

'Elliott has nothing in that chalet, Helena.'

Uh-oh— *Helena*. Reason had always been her friend in the face of *mother voice*. 'The chalets are practically five-star, and I'm sure he has a full wallet.' *And an expense account.* 'He could have easily taken himself for a restaurant meal.'

'When we can offer a home-cooked one instead?'

'He went out anyway. He might as well have eaten in Mitchell's Cliff.' In fact she'd been sure that was what he was doing as the crunch of his tyres on the driveway had diminished.

'I'm less concerned with what he does than with what *we* do. Extending Morgan courtesy to our guest.'

Laney opened her mouth to protest further but then snapped it shut again as feet sounded on the mat outside. An uncontrollable dismay that she hadn't so much as combed her windswept hair washed over her.

But too late now.

'He's coming,' her father announced moments later.

Elliott had clearly paused in the doorway and was greeting a dozing Wilbur, which meant his disturbed *man scent* had time to waft ahead. Wow, he smelled amazing. The same base tones as before, yet different somehow. Spicier. Cleaner.

Tastier.

Heat burbled up under her shirt at the thought, but it was true. Whatever he was wearing was tickling the same senses as the stew still simmering in its own heat on the table.

'Thank you for the invitation, Mr and Mrs Morgan—'

'Ellen and Robert, please, Elliott.'

He stepped up right next to her. 'I nicked out to pick this up. Couldn't come empty-handed.'

Another waft of deliciousness hit her as a bottle clacked against the timber at the centre of the big table.

'Oh, lovely. That's a terrific local winery—Helena's favourite.'

'Really? I didn't know.'

His voice was one-tenth croak, subtle enough that maybe she only heard it because he was standing so close. But he wasn't looking at her, she could tell. Plus, she wouldn't be looking at him if their situations were reversed. On pain of death.

Her mother laughed. 'How could you know?'

Was he worried that she might read something into that? Laney spoke immediately to put the ridiculous idea out of the question. 'You're either a man of excellent taste or Natty Marshall did a real sell-job on you at the cellar.'

'She was pretty slick,' he admitted.

'Sit down, Elliott.' Her mother mothered. 'You look very nice.'

The reassuring way she volunteered that opinion made Laney wonder whether he was worrying at the edges of his shirt or something.

'He's changed into a light blue Saturday night shirt, Laney.'

Oh, no...

'Mum likes to scene-set for me,' she explained, mortified, and then mumbled, 'sorry.'

'Blue shirt, jeans, and I combed my hair,' he added, amusement rich in his low voice.

Was that a statement about *her* wild locks? Her hand went immediately to them.

Her mother continued to be oblivious. 'Sit, too, Laney.'

She did, moving to the left of her chair just as he moved to the right of his. They collided in the middle. She jerked back, scalded.

'Sorry,' he murmured. 'Ladies first.'

'We'll be standing all night if we wait for one of those,' she quipped, still recovering from the jolt of whatever the heck that was coming off him, and then she slid into her seat, buying a moment of recovery time as he moved in next to her.

So that was her question answered. She'd felt the

strength of his torso against hers. He was solid, but definitely not overweight. Not as youthfully hard as her twin, but not soft either. Just right.

Which pretty much made her Goldilocks, snuggling down into the sensation.

The necessity to converse was forestalled by the business of filling plates with stew and side plates with thickly sliced bread and butter.

'Home-made bread?' Elliott asked. Such a charmer. So incredibly transparent.

'Organically grown and milled locally and fresh out of my oven.'

'It's still warm.'

The reverence in his voice surprised a chuckle out of Laney. 'Are ovens not hot in the city?'

An awkward silence fell over the whole table. She didn't need to see her mother's face to know it would be laden with disapproval.

But chivalry was clearly alive and well. 'Bread starts out hot, yes,' he admitted. 'But it's not usually hot by the time it gets to the consumer. This is my first truly home-made loaf.'

The fact that he needed to compensate for her bluntness at all made her twitchy. And just a little bit ashamed. Plus it made her wonder what kind of city upbringing he'd had never to have had fresh-baked bread before. 'Well, wait until you taste the butter, then. Mum churns it herself.'

And bless her if her mother didn't join her daughter in the age-old act of making good. 'Well, I push the button on the machine and then refrigerate the results.'

'You guys seem pretty self-sufficient here…'

And off they went. Comfortably reclining in a topic she knew her parents could talk about underwater—organic farming and self-sustainability. Long enough to give her time to compose herself against the heat still coming off the man to her left as they all tucked into the chicken.

Okay, so he was a radiator. She could live with that. And enough of a city boy to never have had home-baked bread. That just meant they came from different worlds. Different upbringings. She'd met people from outside of the Leeuwin Peninsula before. There was no reason to be wound up quite this tight.

She slid her hand along the tablecloth until her fingertips felt the ring of cool that was the base of the glass of wine her father had poured from the bottle Elliott had contributed. She took a healthy swallow and sighed inwardly at the kiss of gentle Merlot against her tongue.

'Still as good as you remember?' Elliott murmured near her left ear. Swirling more man scent her way.

Okay, this was getting ridiculous. Time to focus. 'Always. We have hives at their vineyard. I like to think that's why it's so good.'

'This wine was fertilised by Morgan's bees?'

'Well, no.' Much as she'd love to say it had been. 'Grape pollen is wind-borne. But we provide the bees to fertilise their off-season cropping. So the bees help create the soil that make their wines so great.'

'Do they pay?'

Back to money. *Sigh.* 'No. They get a higher grape yield and we get the resulting honey. It's a win-win.'

He was silent for a moment, before deciding, 'Clever.'

The rush of his approval annoyed her. It shouldn't make her so tingly. 'Just standard bee business.'

'So tell me about your focus on organic methods,' he said to the table generally. 'That must limit where you can place hives or who you can partner with?'

'Not so much these days,' her father grunted. 'Organics is very *now.*'

'Yet you've been doing it for three decades. You must have been amongst the first?'

'Out of necessity. But it turned out to be the best thing we could have done.'

'Necessity?'

Every cell in Laney's body tightened. This wasn't the first time the topic had come up with strangers, but this was the first time she'd felt uncomfortable about its approaching. The awkward silence was on the Morgan side of the table, and the longer it went on the more awkward it was going to become.

'My eyes,' she blurted. 'My vision loss was a result of the pesticides we were using on the farm. Once we realised how dangerous they were, environmentally, we changed to organic farming.'

Her father cleared his throat. 'And by *we* she means her mother and I. Laney and Owen weren't even born yet.'

She was always sure to say 'we'. Her parents took enough blame for her blindness without her adding to it.

'None of us really knew what they were doing to our bodies,' her father went on, 'let alone to our unborn children.'

Well, one of them, anyway. Owen seemed to have got away with nothing worse than a teenager's attention span.

'Have we made you uncomfortable, Mr Garvey?' her mother said after moments of silence. 'Helena said we should have just sent you to town for a meal...'

Heat rushed up Laney's cheeks as his chair creaked slightly. It wasn't hard to imagine *Oh, really?* in the voice that washed over her like warm milk.

'No. I'm just thinking about how many worse ways the chemical damage might have manifested itself. How lucky you were.'

Again the silence. But this time it wasn't awkward. Surprised was the closest word for the half-caught breath that filled the hush. Was he being intensely dismissive of her loss—and her parents'—or did he actually get it?

And possibly *her*.

Warmth swelled up in her chest, which tightened suddenly. 'Most people wouldn't consider it luck,' she breathed. 'But as it happens I agree with you.'

'And, as threatening as it must have been for you at the time, the decision sealed Morgan's fate. Put you well ahead of everyone else in organics today. It was smart.'

'It was a life-changer in more ways than one,' her mother cut in.

Silence again. Laney filled it with the first thing that entered her mind. 'I gather we'll be seeing you again, Elliott?'

Elliott. The very name tingled as it crossed her tongue.

'Really?' His voiced shifted towards her father. 'You're happy to have me back?'

Robert Morgan was predictably gruff. He always was when he dwelled on the bad old days. 'Yes. I would like to hear what you have to say.'

It didn't take a blind person to catch his leaning on the word 'I'.

'And what about you, Laney? You'll be doing all the escorting.'

'Free advice is my favourite kind. I'll be soaking it up.' But just in case he thought he was on a winner, she added, 'And weighing it up very carefully.'

Approval radiated outwards. Or was it pleasure? Either way she felt it. It soaked under her skin and did a bang-up job of warming her from the inside out as he spoke gruffly.

'That's all I ask.'

Three hours later they walked together back towards the chalet, an unharnessed Wilbur galloping in expanding arcs around them, her hand gently resting on Elliott's forearm. Not entirely necessary, in truth, because she walked this trail often enough en route to the hilltop hives. But she just knew walking beside him would be the one time that a rock would miraculously appear on the trail, and going head-over-tail really wasn't how she wanted him remembering her.

'It's a beautiful night,' he murmured.

'Clear.' *Ugh, such verbal brilliance. Not.*

'How can you tell?'

'The cicadas don't chirp when it's overcast, and I can't smell moisture in the air.'

'Right.'

She chuckled. 'Plus it may be autumn, but it's still summery enough that the odds are on my side.'

He stopped, gently leading her to a halt too. 'Listen, Laney' he said, low and somewhat urgent. 'I don't want every conversation we have to be laden with my reticence to ask you about your vision loss. I want to focus on your processes.'

Was that his way of saying he didn't want to look like an idiot in front of her any more than she did in front of him? Her breath tightened a tiny bit more.

'Why don't you just ask me now? Get it out of the way.'

'Is that okay?'

'I'll let you know if it's too personal.' She set off again, close to his side, keeping contact between their arms but not being formally guided.

He considered his first question for a moment. 'Can you see at all?'

'No.'

'It's just black?'

'It just…isn't.'

Except for when she looked at the sun. Then she got a hazy kind of glow in the midst of all that nothing. But she wasn't even sure she wasn't making that up in response to the warmth on her face. Because she sometimes got a glow with strong emotion too.

'It's like…' How to explain it in a way that was meaningful? 'Imagine if you realised one day that all other human beings had a tail like Wilbur's but you didn't. You'd know what a tail was, and where it went and what its function was, but you just couldn't conceive of what it would be like—or feel like—to have one. The extra weight. The impact on your balance. The modifications you'd need to allow for it. Useful, sure, but not something you can't get by without. That's vision for me.'

'It hasn't held you back at all.'

'Is that a question or a statement?'

'I can see that for myself. You are more accomplished than many sighted people. You don't consider it a disability?'

'A bat isn't disabled when it goes about its business. It just manages its environment differently.'

Silence.

'Are you glaring or thinking?'

'I'm nodding. I agree with you. But there must be things you flat-out can't do?'

'Dad made sure I could try anything I wanted—' and more than a few things she hadn't particularly wanted '—so, no, there's not much that I can't do at all. But there's a lot of things I can't do with any purpose or point. So I generally don't bother.'

'Like what?'

'I can drive a vehicle—but I can't drive it safely or to a destination so why would I, other than as a party trick? I can take a photograph with a camera, but I can't look at it. I can write longhand, but I really don't need to. That kind of thing.'

'Do you know what colours are?'

'I know what their purpose is. And I know how they're different in nature. And that they're meaningful for sighted people. But, no, I can't create colour in my head.'

'Because you've never seen it.'

'Because I don't think visually.'

'At all?'

'When I was younger Dad opened up the farm to city kids from the Blind Institute to come and have farm stays. As a way of helping me meet more children like myself. One of them had nothing mechanically wrong with her eyes—her blindness was caused by a tumour in her visual cortex and that meant she couldn't process what her eyes were showing her perfectly well. But the tumour also meant she couldn't think in images or conceptualise something she felt. She really was completely blind.'

'And that's not you?'

'My blindness is in my retinas, so my brain creates things that might be like images. I just don't rely on them.' She wondered if his pause was accommodating a frown. 'Think of it like this... Mum said you're quite handsome. But I can't imagine what that means without further information because I have no visual frame of reference. I don't conceive of people in terms of the differences in their features, although I obviously understand they *have* different features.'

'How do you differentiate?'

'Pretty much as you'd imagine. Smell, the sound of someone's walk, tangible physical features like the feel of someone's hand. And I have a bit of a thing for voices.'

'How do you perceive me?'

Awkwardness swilled around her at his rumbled question, but she'd given him permission to ask and so she owed him her honesty. 'Your strides are longer than most when you're walking alone.' Though, with her, he took pains to shorten them. 'And you smell—' *amazing* '—distinctive.'

That laugh was like honey squeezing out of a comb.

'Good distinctive or bad distinctive?'

She pulled up as he slowed and reached out to brush the side of her hand on the rough clay wall of the chalet for orientation. 'Good distinctive. Whatever you wear is…nice.'

In the way that her favourite Merlot was just 'nice'.

'You don't do the whole hands-on-face thing? To distinguish between physical features?'

'Do you feel up someone you've just met? It's quite personal. Eventually I might do that if I'm close to someone, just to know, but ultimately all that does for me is create a mind shape, address a little curiosity. I don't rely on it.'

'And people you care about?'

Did he think you couldn't love someone without seeing them?

She pressed her fingers to her chest. 'I feel them in here. And I get a surge of…it's not vision, exactly, but it's a kind of *intensity*, and I experience it in the void where my vision would be when I think about my parents or Owen or Wilbur. And the bees. Their happy hum causes it.'

And the sun, when she stared into it. Which was often, since her retinas couldn't be any more damaged.

'That sometimes happens spontaneously when I'm with someone, so I guess I could tell people apart by the intensity of that surge. But mostly I tell people apart by their actions, their intentions. That's what matters to me.'

'You looked me right in the eye after we shook hands.'

'Only after you spoke. I used the position of your hand and your voice to estimate where your eyes would be. And the moment either one of us moved it wouldn't have worked until I recalibrated. I don't have super powers, Elliott.'

His next silence had a whole different tone to it. He was absorbing.

'You've been very generous with your information, considering what an intrusion my questions are. But it felt important for me to understand. Thank you, Laney.'

'It's no more an intrusion than me asking you what it's like being tall.'

'How do you—? The angle of my voice?'

'And the size of your hand when I shook it. Unless you have freakishly large hands for the rest of your body?'

'No. My hands are pretty much in proportion to the rest of me.'

Cough.

Not awkward at all…

Wilbur snuffling in the distance and the chirpy evening cicadas were the only sounds around them. The only ones Elliott would hear, anyway.

'I'm tall because my father was a basketball player,' he volunteered suddenly. 'It means I spend my days looking at the bald spots of smaller men and trying very hard not to look down the cleavages of well-built women. My growth spurt at thirteen meant I made the school basketball team, and that was exclusively responsible for turning my high school years from horror to hero. It taught me discipline and focus, sharpened my competitiveness and gave me a physical outlet.' He took a breath. 'Without that I'm not sure what kind of a man I might have grown into.'

His words carried the slightest echo of discomfort, as if they were not things he was particularly accustomed to sharing. And she got the sense that he'd just given her a pretty fair trade.

She palmed the packed earth wall of the chalet and opened her mouth to say *Well, this is you*, but as she did so she stepped onto a fallen gum nut loosed by the wildlife foraging in the towering eucalypts above and her ankle began to roll. Her left fingernails bit into the chalet's rammed earth and her right clenched the fabric of Elliott's light jacket, but neither did much to stop her leg buckling.

The strong arm that slid around her waist and pulled her upright against his body was infinitely more effective at stopping her descent.

'Are you okay?' he breathed against her hair.

Other than humiliated? And way too comfortable in his strong hold. 'Occupational hazard' she said, when she really should have been thanking him. 'Happens all the time.'

He released her back onto two feet and waited a heartbeat longer as she tested her ankle for compliance. It held.

'I'm sorry, Laney. Guess I don't have Wilbur's years of training as a guide.'

Guilt saturated the voice that had been so warm just moments before. And that seemed an ungrateful sort of thanks for his catching her before she sprawled onto the ground at his feet.

'It wasn't you. My bottom and hip are peppered with bruises where I hit the dirt. Regularly.'

Talking about body parts suddenly felt like the most personal conversation she'd ever had, and it planted an image firmly between them that seemed uncomfortably provocative.

She released his jacket from between her clenched fingers. 'Thank you for those basketball-player reflexes.'

'You're welcome,' he breathed, and his smile seemed richer in the silence of evening. 'Are you okay to get yourself back?'

She whistled for Wilbur, who bounded to her side from out of the night, and then forked two fingers to touch his furry rump in lieu of a harness. 'Yep. I'm good. I walk these paths every day.'

Not that you'd know it by the wobble in her gait.

Then she set off, turning for the house, and Wilbur kept careful pace next to her, making it easy to keep up her finger contact with his coat. But she wasn't entirely ready to say goodnight yet, although staying was out of the question. Something in her burned to leave him with a better impression of her than her being sprawled, inelegant and grasping, in his arms.

So she turned and smiled and threw him what she hoped was a witty quip back over her shoulder.

'Night. Sorry about the possums!'

CHAPTER FOUR

I<small>T WASN'T THE</small> possums that had kept him up half the night, though they'd certainly been having a ball, springing across his chalet's roof in a full-on game of midnight marsupial chasey. *Kiss* chasey, judging by some of the sounds he'd heard immediately afterwards.

Because if it *had* been the possums he would have been able to fall asleep when they'd finally moved on to foraging in the trees surrounding the chalets for the evening, instead of lying there thinking about the gentle brush of Laney's fingers on his arm, the press of her whole body against his when he'd caught her. The cadence of her laugh.

Her amazing resilience in the face of adversity.

Except that Laney genuinely didn't see it as adversity. She understood that she experienced the world differently from the rest of her family, her friends, but she was pretty happy with those experiences. The world was just as much her oyster as his.

More so, perhaps, because she was so open to experience.

And right about then his mind had flashed him back to watching her dance, wet and bedraggled and beautiful, down at the cove. Then to an imagined visual of her perfect skin marred by small bruises from falling. And then just her perfect skin, and the all-consuming question of whether that dusting of freckles might continue beyond the hem of her dress.

And any hope of sleep had rattled out of the chalet to join the possums.

Pervert.

As if he'd never seen a pretty woman before. Or held one.

Did it even count as holding if you were the only thing stopping someone from falling unceremoniously on their arse? It was more community service than come-on, right?

Elliott shook off the early-morning tiredness and wiped his loafers on the Morgans' mat. But he only had one foot done before the door opened and Laney stood there, resplendent in white overalls straight off the set of *Ghostbusters*.

Except he couldn't remember Murray or Ackroyd ever looking this good in theirs.

'I feel underdressed,' he commented.

Laney's smile was the perfect accessory. 'You won't miss out. I have a pair for you, too.'

'I take it today's bees aren't as friendly?'

'We're doing a run to check the migrating hives. I prefer the farmers to see us taking it seriously. Preserve the mystery.'

'We?'

'Hey, mate.'

Only a brother would shove past a blind woman in a doorway with quite so little regard. That was what gave him away. That and the fact he was basically a short-haired male version of Laney.

A stupid part of Elliott bristled at seeing Laney treated with such casual indifference, though she barely noticed.

'You must be Owen.' Elliott gripped the proffered palm in his, introducing himself and swallowing back the disappointment that today wasn't going to be all about him and Laney. 'Many hands make light work?'

'Owen and I work together on the remote hives,' she said. 'We're checking two off-sites today.'

If there had been any question that the intimate truce of last night was going to continue today, he'd just had his answer. Laney Morgan was all about business this morning.

'We're going to take the back gate out of our

property so you'll get to see more of Morgan land. Come on.'

She stepped past him and brought a white stick out from behind her leg. The first time he'd seen her with one. The first time he'd actually *thought* of her as blind. And instantly he understood why she didn't use it more often.

'No Wilbur today?'

She swept the stick ahead of her as though it were a natural part of her body, pausing only to slap the folded overalls and hood she'd been clutching towards him.

'Captain Furry-Pants has the day off. I think three guides would be excessive.'

Owen was already in the front of the Morgans' branded utility.

'So what will we be doing today?'

His question paused her just before she turned and felt her way up onto the tray of the truck, and she waited as he clambered up behind her. Once they were both on board, safely wedged between large, empty hives, she knocked twice on the window of the cab and Owen hit the accelerator. Hard.

They lurched up to speed.

'Today we're checking for beetle and propolis. We do these hives once a month.'

'Propo what?'

'Bee spit. They produce it to patch up any tiny holes in their hive and keep bacteria out. Humans use it for everything from treating burns to conditioning stringed instruments. Every one of our hives has a single propolis frame in it and the bees will totally cover it a couple of times in a year. We're exchanging those frames today.'

Bee spit. The potential for new markets was greater than he'd imagined. And as long as those obscure markets were buying, Morgan's was selling.

Man, they were *so* the right client for him.

They rumbled through the back roads of the property between fields full of bright, fragrant wildflowers and then skirted the edges of dense, tall forest.

'National Park,' Laney said when he queried. 'Between it and our own lands, it means our bees have a massive tract to forage in and we can leave hives right on our perimeter.'

The ute hit a dip in the road, sending Helena crashing across his lap. A man could get used to this catching and steadying thing. She slid to sit at right angles instead, bracing her feet and her back on the hives packed either side of them. The move meant she wouldn't lurch into him again—a loss—but it meant her long legs bridged his.

Surprise benefit.

'You really couldn't get a more idyllic location—' he started, over the sound of the motor.

'Thank you. That's what I think.'

He'd been about to add...*for your business,* but is that what she'd meant? Or did she just love and value the property because it was home? She couldn't see its beauty, so what was it, exactly, that she loved about it?

'Someone knew what they were doing when they started farming here.'

'My great-grandfather—though Morgan's was mostly a dairy operation then. Mum and Dad focussed on the apiary side of things when they went organic.'

When their daughter was born sightless.

He filled the rest of the journey with questions about yields and methods and percentile measures and she spoke as comfortably about numbers as she did about bee husbandry. There wasn't a single question she couldn't answer.

'You're being amazingly open today.'

'Given how amazingly closed I was yesterday?'

Well...yeah. Before their big discussion under the half-moon. 'Yesterday I felt sure you were going to send me packing.'

'I see no harm in helping you understand our

business. Besides, I'm under instructions from Dad to be civil.'

Oh. Right. 'Not my natural charm, then?'

The ute lurched again and her hand went out automatically and grabbed the first solid thing she could find. His knee. She released it immediately.

'I tend to distrust charming men, actually. I haven't always had the best experiences with smooth talkers.'

'Why's that?' This had nothing to do with business but he was easily as interested in her answer as in anything else they'd yet discussed.

'Most people don't accept my vision as easily as—' She stopped, crunched her face in a frown and then changed direction.

Had she been about to say *as easily as you*? He struggled against the desire to smile so she wouldn't hear any trace of smugness in his voice.

'People tend to want to either rescue me or show me off. As if dating a blind girl somehow improves their status. Neither of which I appreciate, particularly.'

'You don't think they're asking you out for more... traditional reasons?'

'A high-maintenance blind girl? I don't think so.'

Pfff. 'You're the least high-maintenance person I've ever met.'

'They don't know that when they start sniffing around.'

Okay, whatever had happened to her in the past was clearly still a touchy point. 'Maybe they just want to get to know you? Maybe they're just attracted for regular reasons?'

'Knocked off their feet by my beauty?'

Given she'd never seen a sarcastic facial expression in her life, the one she flashed him now had to be innate. And it was a corker. 'You may not prioritise the visual, Laney, but I can tell you for certain that the rest of the world does.'

'Then that's a bonus for them. Poster child for the vision-impaired and passable to behold.'

'Laney, you're more than passable. You have amazing bone structure.'

The compliment hung out there in space, awkward and impossible to undo. She opted to ride through it as though it was any other conversation. 'Actually, I've heard that before.'

'From a man?' *Wow*—that thought bothered him more than was comfortable.

'From the friend who tattooed eyeliner on me.'

That stopped him flat. He stared at her. At the subtle shaded highlighting around her lashes. 'Your friend tattooed you?'

The eyes in question crinkled with her laugh.

'Kelly was training to be a beautician. She needed subjects to work on. She knew I didn't bother with make-up but she said if I only did one thing, ever, to my face it should be that. So we went for it.'

'Kelly was right. You have beautiful eyes.' Eyes that didn't meet his nearly often enough for his liking. He'd work on that. Make a point of touching her and speaking at the same time. 'But what happened to not thinking in visual terms?'

'I'm still a woman, Elliott. And as you pointed out the rest of the planet is so very visual. I saw no reason to go out of my way to look bad.'

Her hands twitched as if they wanted to go to her hair or face or something. It was very typically female. Very human. And really, really endearing.

'Laney, there's not… There's very little chance that what I'm about to say won't sound like a cheesy come-on, but I want to say it because you are nothing if not stoically honest about everything. I think you deserve the same in return.'

For a woman with limited eye expression, the rest of her face certainly managed to convey her nerves just then. 'Okay…'

'Those lightly made-up eyes, in that totally un-made-up face, are pretty much perfect. I give you my word, as a man, on that.'

Her lips parted in surprise.

'Healthy, natural and young, with eyes straight off a billboard. That's what I see.'

She frowned. 'A what?'

He blinked. 'A billboard?'

'Yeah.'

'It's a giant advertising poster.' He knew she knew about those because she'd commented about her brother's bedroom walls, which were still plastered with posters of grunge bands from his youth. 'As big as the side of a house, mounted on freeways and the sides of high-rises.' And suddenly he realised how it was that she'd never encountered a billboard before. It wasn't just because she was blind. 'Have you ever been to the city, Laney?'

'I went when I was little, for a lot of tests. But, no. Not since then.'

'Have you been off the Leeuwin Peninsula? Out of the district?'

'Not for very long.'

And suddenly those eyes that saw nothing revealed so much more. The subtle change in their shape, the flick away from him. And he realised that after everything she had been prepared to talk about he'd just hit something that she wasn't.

Her homing instinct.

He filed it away for later. 'Anyway...that's a billboard. They tend to plaster beautiful models or hot cars all over them. Sometimes together.'

'And you think I have a billboard face?'

Eyes, technically, but… 'Yes, definitely.'

The left corner of her mouth lifted just slightly. As if she wouldn't allow herself to be pleased about that but a tiny bit had leaked through anyway.

'Do *you*, Elliott?'

Should he be excited that she was curious about him or worried about what the truth might lead to? It crossed his mind to exaggerate—not lie outright but just…embellish. But that felt dishonest and entirely without purpose. 'No. Not me. I'm okay, but nothing poster-worthy.'

'Mum's liberal with the word "handsome", so I really don't know how to imagine you.'

'You want me to describe myself?'

She frowned. 'Yes. For what it's worth.'

'I… Well, you know I'm tall. Six-three, to be exact. I have dark hair—'

'What kind of dark?'

Right. Dark was effectively a colour. Okay, this was trickier than he'd imagined. Not that he'd imagined in a million years he'd be having this conversation.

'Dark like night.' As lame as that sounded… 'And

my eyes are the same colour as that cove where I saw you swimming.'

However she perceived *that*.

She smiled, settled back against the empty hives behind her. 'What else?'

Jeez, this wasn't easy. 'Hang on…' He pulled his phone out and got online.

'What are you doing?'

'I have a corporate photo on our website. I'm going to that.'

'You don't know what you look like?'

'I can't describe myself unless I see me.' He clicked a few more times. 'Okay… So… Hair like night, eyes like your ocean… I have a wide forehead, if not for the bit of hair that flops down over it, fairly dominant brows, but not out of control. Hmmm…apparently I have "Jules Vernian" sideburns.' Then, under his breath, 'Which will be gone by morning.'

Her laugh warmed him straight through.

'Ears?'

'Two.' He grinned for himself more than for her. 'Pretty level, regular size, no real lobe.'

'I'm sure that means something to those who study such things.'

'I hate to imagine. My nose is pretty straight, but there's a slight bump in it where I took a ball to the face back in school. My lips are… Well, I was once told they're "kissable"—whatever that means. There's two of them, too—roughly the colour of… fire, maybe? Though they're not being put to much use in this corporate picture. I look like I've never learned to smile.'

Corporate him looked pretty grim, come to think of it.

'I have more stubble on my face today than in this picture because I'm relaxed, and my beard tends to want to grow further down my neck than I'd like. It's a constant pain.' He clicked his phone to darkness. 'So that's me in a nutshell.'

Her lopsided smile evened out on the right and then broke into a fully fledged, fully glorious thing. 'I'm glad you're relaxed with us.'

So was he. She had no idea how rare a thing that was.

'Want to know what that looks like in my head…?' she offered.

Yes, desperately. 'No. I hate bad news.'

'Heathcliff painted by Picasso.'

His laugh was immediate and genuine. 'That's how you're imagining me?'

'Right now, yes.'

'How do you know how Picasso paints?'

'I told you, Mum likes to scene-set. She has an amazing descriptive vocabulary.'

'And Heathcliff?'

'I'm a big reader.'

'Well…I'll take Picasso's Heathcliff. Happily.'

Her voice turned two shades breathier. 'Want to know how I was imagining you before?'

Something told him he didn't. Yet something else whispered that the next words out of her mouth would be amongst the most important of his life. And his subconscious had never let him down yet.

'Go ahead.'

She tipped her head to the sky and stared into the sun, eyes wide open. Straight into it—just as she had that day on the beach. His immediate urge was to leap across and shield her eyes from the damaging rays. But something in her motion told him she'd been doing this for a long time. And that it was special to her.

She tipped her head back down, towards him. 'When I do that, I get a "ghost". Right up-front, where my vision should be.' Her hand waved in a small arc just above her head. 'That's what the specialists call it. My parents would call it a glow.'

'And you see it?'

Her head shook. 'I *experience* it. It's as much a feeling as a visual thing, and it lasts about thirty seconds. I'm not always sure it's even real or whether it's just my imagination filling in blanks. Because I get it for different people, too.'

He struggled hard not to clear his suddenly thick throat. 'You experience me as a...ghost?'

'Yours is dense.'

'Right...'

Her laugh whipped away on the wind as they sped along between the coast and the trees. 'Not literally. They have frequencies and yours is kind of...thick. Rich. Masculine. Which is stupid, given I have two men in the family.'

One or either of them should be hideously un-comfortable right about now, but he found it hard to be anything other than intrigued. And grateful. 'You make me sound positively mysterious. I think I prefer the ghost to the Picasso.'

'Me, too.'

They rumbled onwards in silence and Elliott looked out at the terrain whizzing past them on the private roads—primarily as an excuse not to look at Laney. Just because she couldn't see him do it there was no excuse to stare.

It occurred to him that Laney Morgan 'saw' things more clearly without ever actually seeing them than he ever had with his twenty-twenty vision. She was all about people's qualities, their goodness and their truth. And he should be worried as all hell about that. Worried that she was going to get to the truth of who he really was: the man beneath the corporate suit, the guy without his desk. Because on his worst days Elliott doubted there was much of a man there at all beneath the trappings of his corporate lifestyle, and that maybe his mother had been right in never pushing him to be more. Maybe she'd seen early what he was too cocky and ambitious to admit.

That there might not be much more of a man to be had.

It would certainly explain the hollow emptiness.

And his blazing desperation to fill it with *stuff.*

Owen pulled the ute to a halt by the barest of clearings in the bush on the side of the road, next to a blue steel gate.

'We're here,' she breathed. 'The Davidson property.'

'It's certainly not as impressive as Morgan's entry.'

'This is the back gate. Their four-year-old is allergic, so the hives are on the farthest corner of their farm.'

Owen pulled through and then closed the gate behind them before driving in low gear up a barely discernible track. He stopped at the top, in a croft of trees, near to two dozen white hives. Elliott pushed to his feet and guided Laney to the back edge of the ute before jumping down ahead of her.

Assisting her seemed the right thing to do, though he knew in his heart she'd probably been jumping down off the back of this truck since she was a kid. She sat on the back edge of the ute and felt for his shoulders as he stepped up between her legs and braced her gently around the waist. Then he lifted as she slid.

Helping her might be appropriate, but there was nothing appropriate about his reaction to her body's slide down his, coming so soon on the tail of yesterday's grope disguised as a rescue. Even through his own clothes his skin immediately questioned what she was wearing below the flimsy safety overalls. A tank top, maybe? Shorts? Didn't feel like much. Instead, as his hands bunched in the light waxy material, all he could feel was heat.

Laney's heat. His own.

She settled more certainly on her feet and tipped her head up on a murmur. 'Thank you.'

'You're welcome.'

And then it happened. Their proximity and the direction of his voice meant she was able to lock those deep grey eyes directly on his and even though his mind knew they were sightless, his heart felt sure that her soul was seeing him.

Right down into his own.

It was as inconceivable as the idea that she saw him as a ghost glow, yet utterly unshakeable.

She *was* seeing him on some level. Whether she knew it or not.

'Suit up, Elliott,' Owen said, slamming his door and moving straight to the side of the ute to unlash the empty hive boxes. 'Heaps to do.'

A pretty flush ran up Laney's jaw and she stepped back. 'Ignore him—everybody does. You're here observing.'

The glance Owen cast his sister was as brief as it was wounded.

'I don't mind helping out. A bit of labour will be good for me,' said Elliott.

'I don't want to be responsible for callousing up those hands.' The colour doubled as she realised what her casual comment was an admission of. 'But it's up to you.'

She turned and walked towards her brother, her knuckles lightly grazing the dirtied edge of the ute, keeping her orientated, and Owen loaded her up with equipment.

Elliott had to bite his tongue. Her brother treated her as if she was as capable as he was—and that was no doubt true—but deep down inside he couldn't shake the feeling that Helena Morgan was someone to be cherished, protected. Spoiled like a princess. He'd thought she was regal in those first moments yesterday and the sense hadn't left him. It was in her carriage. And her confidence. And the way she commanded any space she was in.

And he'd never in his life wanted so badly to cherish someone.

Nor known for certain how unwelcome that would be.

CHAPTER FIVE

IT WAS A full month before Elliott returned to the farm. A few short weeks for Laney to get her headspace and her perspective—and her tranquil existence—back in order.

Nowhere near long enough, judging by the little random rushes of anticipation as the weekend approached. The whole weekend, this time—not just the second half of Saturday and the first half of Sunday. Her mum had told her that Elliott was driving down mid-afternoon Friday, to get ahead of the weekend exodus down south.

She knew his car the moment it began travelling the long drive up to the house. With any other vehicle she'd hear the engine first and the tyre-crunch second. Whatever Elliott drove was close to silent running. Which meant it was expensive. Morgan's generated enough profit that her family could have expensive cars to match their architect-designed house perched high on the bluff, too, if they cared about that sort of thing. But this was a working property, where vehicles were function before form, and nothing here ran silently.

So she knew he was here, and knew he was probably settling in to his chalet—when had it become *his* chalet?—until dinner, and she was determined not to make a big deal of his arrival. Because it wasn't. He was just a visitor.

Despite what the ghost glow urged.

It had come back with a vengeance the moment she'd heard Elliott was returning—so strongly she wondered how she hadn't noticed it diminishing.

Ridiculous.

And just like that she decided to head into town for the evening. She wasn't about to sit through another meal unable to focus on anything but Elliott Garvey. And she wasn't about to indulge her body's insane anticipation, either. It would just have to wait.

She reached for her phone.

'Owen,' she said as soon as her brother answered her call. 'I changed my mind about dinner. How soon can we leave?'

Within the half-hour she was comfortably installed at the Liar's Saloon in Mitchell's Cliff, surrounded by Owen's mates and talking with the younger sister of her best friend. At least, *she* was talking; Kelly's sister seemed to be thoroughly distracted. Only about half of her answers were actually in synch with the conversation.

Laney sighed, giving up. 'So which one is it?'

'Huh?' Kristal asked, still not really attending.

'Which of my brother's mates are you all breathless for?'

Kristal's voice rose a half-octave in a half-croak, half-squeak protest. *'Laney!'*

'Sorry.' She leaned in closer and *faux*-whispered. 'Travis or Richard?'

'What makes you think it's not Owen?'

'Because Owen's *Owen*. He's not distraction-worthy.' And he had no real interests beyond the ocean.

'You say that because he's your brother.'

'I say that because he's a dufus.'

Kristal laughed, overly loud, confirming Laney's worst fears. *Owen.* The man-boy who couldn't keep a girlfriend for five minutes. 'Don't fall for Owen, Kristal. Fall for Travis. He's lovely.'

And Travis was the only one close to Kristal's age.

'I dated him in high school.'

'Oh. What about Rick, then?'

'Meh.'

'What about anyone else in this pub?'

'I don't want anyone else. I want O—'

Kristal's inward gasp was the first giveaway as

the opening vowel of her brother's name morphed into a breathy, 'O*h, hello…*'

The certain footfalls through the noisy pub were the second.

And Kristal's urgently whispered, 'Incoming!' as a waft of instantly recognisable cologne brushed towards them was final confirmation.

Elliott.

'Owen, good to see you,' that deep voice murmured.

Her brother's chair shifted and palm slapped palm.

'Welcome back, mate,' Owen said, before doing fast introductions around the table. Kristal—typically—gushed and giggled and seemed to forget all about her great infatuation of moments before in the face of a better, more interesting and even less suitable option.

Elliott pulled a chair up next to her with exaggerated movements. 'Laney.'

'Welcome back to the Peninsula. I have a big weekend planned for you.'

'I'm glad to hear it. How have you been?'

'Great. And you?' Every word was a mask for what she really wanted to say. And do. More than anything she wanted to reach out and brush her fingertips across his smooth ones again. In lieu of hello.

'Passable. Busy singing Morgan's praises to the senior partners.'

Oh, joy. 'You *have* remembered that nothing is a done deal, right?'

'Definitely. But in my experience optimism is generally rewarded.'

Laney could practically feel Kristal's speculation, and it must have been just as obvious outwardly because Elliott turned his voice away slightly.

'Kristal, is it? How do you know Laney?'

Once it would have angered her to have every conversation linked back to her. But she recognised it for the strategy it was, reconfirming Elliott as a kind man as well as good, subtly telling Kristal he wasn't interested. Pity Kristal was anything but subtle.

The heavy scent of gardenia wafted off the younger woman's skin as she tossed back her hair. Trademark move. 'Through my sister. They're best friends.'

'Kristal's sister is Kelly,' Laney murmured.

'Ah, the beautician.'

'Ex-beautician.' Kristal was sulky. 'Now shacked up with a farmer in Ireland.'

'You must miss her.'

The slight change in the timbre of his voice told Laney that Elliott was speaking to her. 'We both do.'

'But thank goodness for webcams, hey?' Kristal cut in, bright and overly loud, but in the absence of any kind of response from Elliott her conversation dried right up.

'Kelly did the full backpacking around Europe extravaganza a couple of years ago,' Laney said, mostly for something to say, 'and met Garth in a pub in County Kerry. I always knew I'd lose her to love.'

His chuckle flirted with the fine hairs on her skin. 'You didn't go with her?'

'Backpacking in Europe? Does that seem the sort of thing I might do?'

'I don't see why not.'

'Because she's *blind*,' Kristal pointed out helpfully. In a half-whisper. As if it was some kind of secret. Or maybe a reminder for Elliott.

Actually, Laney wouldn't put that past her. Kristal cheated at board games, too.

He ignored her. 'That doesn't stop you doing anything at home. Why would it be different overseas?'

'I had a business to run.' And it wouldn't have been fair on Kelly, who'd saved her whole working life for the opportunity. And because Laney liked to be independent—which she could be, at home. 'Besides, we get foreign tourists by the busload. Why would I need to leave?'

'Because there's a whole world to discover. People. Places.'

The implication irked. 'Better places? Better people?'

'Different. New. You're missing so much.'

'Surely wherever I went I'd be missing a lot? I might as well stay home and miss it.'

Disbelief puffed from his lips.

'Excuse me,' Kristal announced somewhat sulkily. 'I'm going to talk to Owen.'

Neither of them acknowledged her departure.

'That's quite a theory,' Elliott murmured.

'Feel free to disagree.'

'It seems impolitic to argue with—'

'A blind girl?'

'With the woman I'm relying on to keep an open mind this weekend.'

Oh. Back to business. Of course. 'I'll be sure to trade on that as fully as I can, then.'

'You should.' A smile enriched his words. 'It won't last for ever.'

'Have *you* travelled overseas?'

'Of course.'

As if it was automatically such a given. 'Why?'

'To see the world. To get a better understanding of my place in it.'

'How old were you?'

Maybe on someone else his pause would simply have been swallowed by the pub music. But to her it practically pulsed.

'I first went overseas when I was seventeen.'

'Seriously? Can you even get a passport before you're of age?'

'With parental consent.'

'And your mother let you go?'

'Eventually. It took me a year of campaigning. But I wore her down.'

'You wanted to go at sixteen?'

'I wanted to go at *thirteen*, but the law said I had to wait until I was sixteen.'

'Why so young?'

As always, he gave his answer actual thought. Laney filled the silence soaking up his scent.

'Because it was all there waiting for me.'

'And you couldn't wait for *it*?'

'I convinced myself I'd be missing something. And the only thing stopping me seeing it was my mother.'

'Could she not afford it?'

'She never travelled.'

Something in his tone tightened her chest. 'That's not actually a crime, Elliott.'

'My mother was free to make her own choices. I was trapped, unable to choose until I was sixteen. I hated that.'

'Having to wait?'

'Having to ask. Being reliant on someone who was never going to take me out of the state, let alone the country.'

'You never went anywhere as a kid?'

'We went on a grand total of one family holiday in my whole life. I drove further getting here to you.'

Getting to you. She forced the little thrill of those words down. He meant Morgan's. Of course he did. But still…

'So you headed off to see the world. How did you pay for it?'

'I'd been working after school in a fast food place since I was fourteen, I saved up enough for the first leg of my journey as soon as I left school.'

'To where?'

'Cheapest flight out of Perth was to Bali. You'd be amazed at how many people go to the trouble of travelling to another country and then don't want to engage with the locals. I ran errands for xeno-phobic Westerners for a few months before hopping over to Vietnam, then Thailand and India. Picking up whatever work I could get, always living local. Living cheap. Exploiting whatever opportunities I could find as I went along. Country-hopping.'

'How did you manage the languages? The politics in some of those areas? As a kid?'

'I didn't always, but I got by. By the time I hit India I had a system and I was of age. Bars, hotels and restaurants were perfect for short-term work, because you could sneak at least one decent meal a day while getting paid. I kept a low profile and always kept moving.'

'You didn't want to stop?'

'No.' Passion leaked out of him as a groan. 'I'd been stopped my whole life. I just wanted to move.'

She shuffled around towards him. 'Then why did you come home?'

When she said 'home' it was with a respectful breath. But she got the sense that to Elliott it was more of a dirty word.

He accepted a drink from the waiter who had delivered it to their cluster of seats and then dropped his voice down for her hearing only.

'I grew up. Got tired of my own pace. And I realised that I could get the same spirit of...*conquering*...from finding small businesses and growing them. Selling for a profit. Eventually, that led to a buy-sell pattern that was as nomadic as my travelling but more profitable, and Ashmore Coolidge took me on as an intern. And the rest is history.'

What he saw as nomadism she saw as reluctance to commit. Not that it had made him any less money that way. 'No more travel?'

'For business, yes. And the odd holiday back to Bali, where it all started.'

'We're very different people,' she murmured.

The only part of his wanderlust that she could relate to was the frustration towards a parent. She'd felt it her whole life, but attached to her over-eager father, whereas Elliott's had been with his apparently under-achieving mother.

'Not so different. You wouldn't have grown Morgan's the way you have if you didn't have a pioneering spirit.'

'I grew it to secure our financial base. I wasn't looking to revolutionise the industry.'

'Yet you have in some ways.'

'What ways?'

'The apitoxin side of your business. Treating rheumatism and Parkinson's. That's pretty unusual. The surf wax.'

Hmm. Someone had been reading up.

'Apitoxin is not revolutionary. I started with bee venom in response to the Davidsons' allergic son—

to help desensitise him so that they can stay on the land they love.'

And once she'd discovered that harvesting the venom didn't have to kill the bees, she'd realised it was a perfect by-product of what they did every day, anyway.

'And we produce near one of Australia's best surf regions. Of course we were going to make a speciality board wax. But I still didn't invent the idea.'

'There's nothing that Morgan's is doing that's totally unique? What about your facial recognition work?'

Really? Was he going to keep badgering until she confessed to being the Steve Jobs of bees? 'It's *the bees* that are amazing. And the software engineers. Not me.'

'It was your proposal.' But something in her expression must have finally dawned on him. 'Why don't you want to be amazing, Laney?'

Frustration hissed out of her. 'Because I'm not. I'm just me. Anything I do is out of curiosity or the desire to strengthen our brand. I'm not curing cancer or splitting atoms.'

'Not yet…'

Ugh..! 'Why does everyone try to make me more than I am? I just work with bees. They are my business and I try to be smart about business. But that's it.'

'Laney—'

'We have a whole weekend ahead of us, and I'm not going to show you anything of interest if you don't let this go. Your visit is about Morgan's—not about me.'

'Okay, take it easy. I'll drop the subject. But at some point you're going to have to accept what everyone else knows—that you *are* Morgan's.'

You are *Morgan's.*

She wasn't. She didn't want to be. She was *a* Morgan and that was it. Morgan's was a family, a plural, a heritage and a way of life. It was the genetic memory and the learning of everyone who'd ever had anything to do with their bees, going right back as far as their founder, her great-grandfather, and that first Queen he'd hived up as a hobby.

She and Morgan's were as symbiotic as queens and their colonies: one couldn't exist without the other. But, as reverent as they were while the Queen lived, ultimately when she was lost the colony just made a new one. They kept the hive strong.

It wasn't personal with bees.

So why was Elliott trying to personalise this? Why was he trying to hang Morgan's success around her neck, all millstone-ish? And why was he working his way up to making Morgan's continued success contingent somehow on her...what had he called it...?

Her pioneering spirit.

As if that was a prerequisite for something to come.

'Good morning.'

Wilbur slowed her to a halt halfway to the chalet. 'Morning, Elliott. Sleep well?'

'I slept brilliantly. May I?'

How did she know what he was asking? Yet she did. 'Sure.'

She unclipped her harness and gave Elliott the moment he'd asked for with Captain Furry-Pants. Released, Wilbur knew he was allowed to enjoy it. Just be a dog. The two of them enjoyed a mutual rough-house until they naturally parted, all done.

She buckled up the harness again and Wilbur sat at attention by her leg. 'No possums this time?'

'Nothing I didn't sleep through.'

Bully for him. She'd slept as badly as those possums. 'Have you had breakfast?'

'I've had coffee. Close enough.'

'That might work for you in the city, but here a coffee doesn't fuel you until morning tea. You'd better have a reasonable lunch.'

'Yes, ma'am.'

She tipped her head. 'I don't want to have to carry you if you faint.'

His chuckle carried them across the paddock. 'So what's the plan for this morning?'

'I thought I'd show you where we make the queens and the Royal Jelly. Two more of our sidelines.'

'You *make* the queens?'

'Well, the bees do it. We just give them a nudge.'

Elliott followed Laney and Wilbur between fences and along the crunch of a gravel path towards the plant sector. Inside, a pair of workers chatted to each other over the *whirr-whirr* of the centrifuge harvester as they worked. It was exactly per the videos Elliott had watched for research. But over in the corner progress was more silent and studied. And that was where Laney was leading him.

If she'd walked him off a cliff he'd have considered following.

Which went to show how desperate he'd become in his hunt for the meaning of life.

'Hi, Laney.' Two voices piped up at the same time.

Laney introduced them and then launched into presentation mode.

'So, when the Queen is ready to step down, she creates special cells and her attendants know to pack them with super-nutritious jelly instead of honey.' She ran her long fingers along the work her staff were doing until she found the enlarged cells. 'It's the exclusive diet of Royal Jelly which produces a fertile virgin queen instead of an infertile worker bee. Hence the name.'

The way she said it—with such a *ta-da!* in her voice… It made him wish he hadn't already done so much reading up. That way her passion could infect him for real. 'So you place artificial cells in the hive and the attendants just fill it? No questions asked?'

She passed him a row of artificial queen cups to examine. 'Bees aren't good with the big picture. And this is the most important moment in their bee career. Thousands of bees will be born and die without ever facing such responsibility.'

Jeez—if he'd waited for opportunities to come to him he'd have withered and died right there in his tiny alley-facing office.

'So a new queen hatches and the hive is happy ever after?'

Her laugh was overly loud even in the busy plant. 'No, multiple virgin queens emerge and fight to the death until only the strongest is left standing.'

Okay, that hadn't been in any of his pre-reading. 'That's very…Machiavellian.'

'Once the victor emerges she has a couple of days

to gather her strength and then she mates with as many drones from unrelated hives as she can in a day in a special yard we set up.'

'Bloodied and hepped up on battle frenzy? I'm amazed she gets any takers at all.'

'The drones are highly motivated. Every egg a queen will ever produce in her lifetime comes from that single blazing day of sexual excess.'

'When I come back I want to be a drone,' he said. 'Sounds like they have it best.'

'Sure. If you don't mind getting your genitals torn out for your troubles.'

His, *'Sorry...?'* was more of a choke.

'When the drone yard is littered with disembowelled corpses she flies back to her starter hive and then lays for the rest of her months-long life.'

Lucky she couldn't see his gape.

'I thought you were this gentle, sweet farm girl. I take it all back. You are as ruthless as they come, Helena Morgan.'

She didn't look the slightest bit put out—if anything she looked pleased. 'Surely that's a compliment, coming from you? Besides, if you don't like that then maybe we shouldn't show you how Royal Jelly is produced.'

'What could possibly top pimping, disembowelment, sanctioned orgies and virgins fighting to the death?'

One of Laney's staff busied himself melting the wax seal on the rest of the queen cells with a heat lamp and then scooped out the Royal Jelly onto the edge of a collection container, plucked a tiny grub out and squashed it on the table.

Laney's face was comically grave. 'Bee-o-cide.'

For some reason that shocked him more than anything else she'd done or said. In his mind Laney was as peace-and-love as any hippy, so bee-slaughter didn't sit comfortably. 'But you go to so much trouble to save the other bees?'

'Has it only just dawned on you that we're farmers, Elliott? These ones would have fought to the death anyway. We just pre-pick the survivor.'

'So you play God?'

'They're essentially clones. The ethics get a little murky. Besides, the grubs are tiny when they're swamped in Royal Jelly. Virtually insentient.'

'Wow.' He shook his surprise free. 'Here I was, feeling sorry for the worker bees who slave away keeping the voracious Queen and her royal young in riches, but I think they might actually have the best of the lot. They spend their days seeing the world, scooping up nectar in the warm sunshine, stretching their wings.'

Her pretty face tightened. 'I thought you would have identified more with the Queen.'

'Why?'

'Entombed in your office cell. Growing large on gathered riches. Fighting for supremacy against your colleagues until you run the show and then working yourself to death until you either create your own replacement or someone knocks you off.'

That dismal view of Ashmore Coolidge really wasn't all that far off reality. On its worst days. 'You make my job sound a lot more exciting than it is. I just sit in an office and try to be smart.'

'Bees have a system. It's worked for them for a very long time. We don't mess with it—we just work with it. And we birth a heck of a lot more bees than we kill.'

And this *was* a farm, after all. Primary production. They did the dirty work so the rest of the country could eat. Had he really expected it to include no death at all just because it was bees and not beef?

He watched the process a few times over and got a sense of how fast the two employees could work, how many queens could be created in a day, and how much Royal Jelly was harvested. Then he multiplied that by the number of hives their production report said were in play at any one time and the number of times a year that this process happened to the same hive.

'That's a lot of jelly in a year.' At a small fortune per kilo. Sticky gold. 'What do you do with all the Queens?'

His unease about Laney's straight-faced acceptance of bee-o-cide couldn't outlast his curiosity. His mind buzzed with thoughts of global expansion potential and operational ramifications. An increasing number of northern hemisphere countries were losing entire apiaries as their winters worsened. Southern hemisphere breeders could ship them new hives, ready to go in spring and keep their agriculture alive.

The possibilities, the income—and Ashmore Coolidge's commission—were endless.

'Come on—show me the honey extraction.'

CHAPTER SIX

LANEY HAD BEEN right about breakfast. He should
have eaten before starting. It wasn't even noon yet
and he was flagging already.

'I blame it on the country air,' he grumbled when
she queried his increasing quietness.

'You're standing in a shed full of energy.'

'I can't eat the honey your staff have gone to so
much trouble to extract.'

'No. But you can eat honey that *you've* gone
to trouble to extract. Come on. I'll show you our
smallest sideline.'

Two sun-bleached girls—one brunette, one Nor-
dic-looking—sat with a plastic crate of fresh honeycomb between them, squeezing the honey out
by hand.

'Here,' Laney said, nudging an empty stool with
her foot. She pulled another over from the corner
and sat it next to his.

The Nordic girl handed him a chunk of whole
messy honeycomb, complete with the odd bee
carcass.

'Have you ever milked a cow?' Laney asked.

Of course he hadn't. That would have required a normal childhood visit to a farm. But she couldn't see his pointed look so he was forced to reconsider his sarcasm.

'No.'

'Okay, then. Um…have you ever caught a fish?'

'Yes.' That he *had* done. He and Danny on *Misfit*. Though, to be fair, their boat trips were more about talking and drinking than any concerted effort at catching a fish.

'Okay, so harvesting honey manually is the same kind of slow, steady action as when you're running a fishing line. Squeeze, release. Squeeze, release.' She demonstrated on thin air.

He glanced at the girl next to him, got a sense of the action and then tried it. A chunk of his honeycomb immediately came away and fell into the collection container—wax and all—with a dull thud.

'Too hard.' Laney laughed and bent to retrieve it before squeezing its honey free herself. 'Squeeze… release…' she repeated, and then leaned half over him to place her hands around his. 'Here, like this…'

Her strong fingers closed gently around his which, in turn, closed much less gently around the honeycomb. Instantly he got a sense of how light his touch had to be.

'Squeeze...' She did so and it was steady and gentle, yet oddly firm at the same time. 'And release...'

Releasing came with a slight twist of her wrists that somehow compelled the honey out of the comb while keeping the waxy parts more or less in hand. She repeated both motions again, brushing more fully against him on the 'squeeze' and then retreating slightly on the 'release'.

The action definitely reminded him of something, but it sure as heck wasn't fishing. And he sure as heck shouldn't be thinking about it now. But with Laney this close, all clean and warm and stretched across him as she was, it was hard to think of anything else.

'You do this manually?' He forced words from his lips just as she was doing with the honey from the honeycomb. Just to return some normality to this highly charged moment. 'Why?'

'It's good training for new staff, but there's also a small market for naturally harvested honey. Wax, dead bees and all. We sell it as Morgan's Naturále.'

Au naturále was not something he should be thinking about right now any more than the sensual squeeze and release action of Laney's hands coiled so intimately around his. He concentrated on the action, on the accumulating pool of raw honey in the container between his legs, and very much *not* on the earthy woman by his side.

She released his hands and sat back, leaving hers dripping over the collection container while he continued.

Eventually Laney spoke. 'Stasia?'

The girl to his right peered into his bucket and then said in accented English, 'Not bad.'

Stasia tapped another tub with her foot and Elliott tossed the remaining ball of waxy mush in with hers. His hands were honey-coated, like sticky, sweet gloves. Stasia took his container and upended his honey into her own as Laney stood. Elliott automatically turned for the sinks that they'd used before the little demonstration.

'No.' Laney caught him with a gentle body-block, given her hands were as honey-coated as his. Her block meant she brushed into him much harder than she already had. 'That's the whole point.'

'Then how do I get it off?'

'Like this.'

She lifted her hand and moved her lips close to where a rivulet of dark honey ran down her wrist. As he watched her tongue came out and caught it, tracing it back up her wrist to its source. His body responded immediately.

Are you freaking kidding me?

'It's the best bit,' she purred. 'You wanted some energy.'

Ah, no... Energy was not going to be a problem now. His bloodstream was suddenly awash with adrenaline and a dozen hormones designed to get—and hold—his attention. But he followed her lead, sucking the honey off his own fingers one by one, watching her do the same to hers. The warm, sweet goo stuck to his lips—and to hers—exactly as his gaze was bonded to Laney. He fully exploited the opportunity to watch her without her knowing.

He closed his mouth around his own finger as she did the same with hers, the real sweetness merging with the imagined sweetness of what her lips were doing as they made steady work of the honey.

If he timed it just right it was almost as if their two mouths were meeting each other through the sticky goodness. His imagination just about exploded over how amazing that might be.

'Nice, huh?' Stasia said from behind him, reminding him that the two of them weren't *actually* alone in a dark place, kissing the heck out of each other.

'Yeah.' He stumbled back a half-step, breaking Laney's spell. Hopefully she'd chalk that deep husk in his voice to honey appreciation.

'It's jarrah,' Laney said. 'From the state forest

bees. Nothing quite like it.' Her ponytail tilted. 'Have you had enough?'

Nope. Nowhere near. 'Just about.'

He finished the stickiest bits off and then joined Laney at the wash-trough to scrub the rest free. His body cried out at the wasted opportunity. And he'd never taste honey again without remembering the past few minutes.

And Laney.

'So now what?' he asked, when he was sure his voice would hold.

'I wondered if you'd like to see more of the property? To understand its scope?'

Her simple suggestion was saturated with pride. And of course he did. But he would have said yes to just about anything that would have meant more time with Laney.

'That sounds like a bigger job than Wilbur will be up for.'

'Oh, definitely. I only take him up there occasionally. Both of us lack the stamina required.'

He'd beg to differ. Every part of her screamed endurance.

'If you don't mind driving we can take one of the Morgan's utes. I'll pack us a lunch.'

More time alone with Laney. More time to learn about the business—and about her—and food for his hollow stomach into the bargain. It was just a pity she couldn't pack something to fill his empty soul.

'Sounds great.'

'Okay. Let's head back to the house and you can pick up the ute while I throw together something to eat.'

Throw together.

As if this was just a casual thing. As if her heart wasn't doing the whole *Riverdance* thing on her diaphragm.

The ute slowed to a rumbly idle and Elliott turned to her. 'Now where?'

'Is there nothing in front of us but ocean?'

'From here to the horizon.'

'Okay, turn right along the coast track.'

'How far?'

'Until you see dense trees to the north.'

'And to the south?'

'The south is a little sketchy—as you discovered the first day you were here.' The day he'd watched her dancing and being a fool with Wilbur, wading in the water with her skirt hiked up to her hips— all of the above—without realising he was partly on Morgan land.

They turned north onto the coast track and Laney

lowered her window to enjoy the closeness of the sea. It filled the ute's cabin with the smell of ocean and the slight dampness of salty spray.

'You love the ocean?' Elliott asked.

'I love the coast, generally.'

'Well, you certainly picked the right place to grow up, then. It's beautiful.'

She didn't need to agree aloud. Her sigh said it for her.

'How do you experience it?' he risked. 'The coast.'

'I can smell the vastness of the ocean on the air. And the sounds coming off the land are more... muted than the ones from the sea. So, to me, the coast is all about space and open air and beauty and deep, fresh breaths.'

She heard the moment he clicked his teeth closed on whatever he'd been about to say.

'What? Go ahead and ask.'

'It wasn't a question,' he said. 'I just... It saddens me that you'll never see it. So you can see how right you are.'

Don't feel sorry for me...

'Have you ever heard a bee quack?'

As subject-changers went, that was pretty solid. Though hardly subtle.

But she was rewarded with one of Elliott's warm laughs. 'Can't say I have.'

'It's more of a battle cry, really. The first virgin queen to hatch out *toots* to taunt the yet-to-be-born queens and they *quack* back at her from inside their cells, calling her on her challenge and begging to be let out so they can fight her.'

'Uh-huh...'

'But they're not actually making a sound—they're communicating with vibrations. We just hear it as sound because we lack the sensory perception to feel it as vibration.'

'A vibratory Morse code?'

'Yeah. But it doesn't make the experience any less real for us because we hear it as sound. It's just a different way of perceiving the same thing. I'm no more deprived by not seeing something than the bees are by not hearing their own toots. We both still experience it.'

'Wouldn't you like someone to experience the world your way sometimes?'

No one had ever asked her that before. They were usually more concerned about *her* sharing *their* experiences. 'Can any of us ever truly share our own perceptions? I've had other blind kids here and even we didn't experience things the same way.'

'Maybe not.'

'My joys and disappointments are as relative as yours. I get more pleasure from the ocean than just about anything else. I get the least pleasure from thinking about the day I'll need to let Captain Furry-Pants go. And there are a thousand differentials in between.'

'Really? Your dog more than your family?'

'Any of them will break my heart, of course, but Wilbur… He has meant freedom and trust—' *and love* '—for me for so long. I know that's going to be a really, really bad day.'

Vulnerability saturated her voice and she wondered what he'd do with it.

'I get it, you know. Why you get tired of people focussing on your blindness.'

'Actually, that's not it. Not exclusively anyway. I just…'

'Just what?'

'*Ugh.* This whole conversation is harder because of what you do.'

'Realising?'

'It's your job to look at things in terms of their potential.'

'You don't want me looking at your potential?'

'No.' *Because that means you're not looking at me.* 'Because people are more than just the sum of their achievements.'

'Yeah. But I'm not paid to assess how nice people are. I'm trained to look at what they've done and what they still could do.'

Right. She did somehow manage to keep forgetting that. This was *work* for him. 'So what happens to the businesses you work with that aren't realising their potential? Or that have none?'

'I cut them free. Find something with more return on the investment of my time.'

The implication tugged at her heart hard enough to hurt. 'Does that go for people, too?'

His silence was filled with a frown.

She tried a different approach. 'Tell me... Do you have any ordinary friends?'

'Depends what you mean by "ordinary".'

'Do you have any friends who aren't high achievers, or leaders in their field, or go-getters like you?'

'No. But the world I live in tends to be filled with high achievers. We all move at the same pace.'

Just like the bees. All one frequency. And someone new to the hive had to match it or get out of the way.

'Do you not have a single person in your life who is just a regular person? With no great ambitions or plans? Someone who just lives the life they are presented with?'

Elliott's snort was immediate. 'You just described my mother.'

'Really? Yet you ended up so different?'

'Thank you.'

Discomfort dribbled like cool water down her spine. But she held her judgement.

He heard it, anyway, in her silence.

'My childhood was not like yours, Laney.'

Not if he'd left the country at the first opportunity, no. 'Was it bad?'

'It wasn't *hell,* but we struggled for everything we had. We existed, with our noses just poking up above the poverty line. And that seemed sufficient for my mother.'

'But it wasn't enough for you?'

'No. It was not. Not when I could see what others had. I always fought to be better. Brighter. More secure.'

'She didn't share your ambition?'

'She did not.'

Anyone else probably wouldn't have heard his quiet words as he turned them out through the far window. But Laney did. Of course she did. She heard the individual pitch differences between two bees—she wasn't going to have any trouble with gravelly tones less than a foot away from her, no matter how whispered.

'I'm sorry.'

'Don't be. I rose above it—got out.'

'No. I meant I'm sorry that you don't have a good relationship with your mother. Mothers are important.'

Silence.

'It's not a bad relationship,' he defended, finally. 'We're just very different. I think I inherited more of my father's traits.'

'Maybe that made things harder for your mother? That you were like him?'

'Don't go imagining that there was a great "love lost" story there, Laney. He was a one-night stand in the village at a Youth Championships meet. There was no great romance.'

'She was an athlete?' Somehow that didn't fit with the passive woman he'd described.

'Gymnast. Until me. Then she just threw it all in.'

Having a kid would do that to a woman's sporting career... But there was real pain beneath all that judgement, so she holstered that opinion, too.

'How old was she?'

'Sixteen.'

'*Wow*. The Garvey family all like to strike out young, then?'

The surprise in his voice was palpable. 'She still lives in the house we were assigned when I was born. She bought it in a state buy-back scheme. How is that striking out?'

Oh… A state housing kid. Suddenly that enormous chip on his shoulder took a more defined shape. 'On her own, with a tiny baby and no father… That's just as courageous as you jetting off to Bali.'

More so, maybe.

The ute wheels rattled on the gravel track. Eventually she accepted that he wasn't going to reply.

'Elliott?'

'I'm processing.'

Not happily, by the sound of it. She felt for his forearm where it rested on the gearstick and laid her hand there. But his sigh didn't sound much relieved. If anything it sounded irritated. Tension saturated his tone.

'Do you know how small I feel for giving an earful of *wahh* about my crappy childhood to a woman who was blind all of hers?'

'My childhood was pretty much great,' she said. 'Yours wasn't. It's okay to comment on that.'

A half-breathed *mmm* was her only answer. And something about it gave her the courage to go beyond what was probably polite.

'Do you love her?'

No answer. But his silence didn't feel like a no. On the contrary.

So she amended. 'Does she love you?'

'As much as she can, given I ruined her life.'

Empathy washed through her in a torrent. 'She told you that?'

'She didn't have to. No way she'd have struggled like we did if I hadn't been part of the picture. She was a world champion. Destined for big things.'

The ghost glow high in her consciousness changed shape then, added depth and complexity. Resembled much more a wounded little boy than a confident man.

He cleared his throat. 'Anyway, enough of my bleating. Do I just keep following this track?'

She knew enough about her brother and father to know when to let something lie. 'Have you hit the crossroad yet?'

'Nope.'

Every instinct wanted to reach out and curl her fingers around his. To lend him her strength. But something told her it wouldn't be welcomed. 'Stop driving like such a nanna. We don't have all day.'

His grudging chuckle fuelled a little boost in speed and they started moving along more steadily. When he slowed the ute again a few minutes later she directed him left.

'Where does this lead?'

'Another lookout. Dad proposed to Mum up here.'

'Really? Are you sure you want to show me somewhere so…personal?'

Why? Did he not want to encourage anything personal between them? 'It's not personal for me. I wasn't even born yet. When Mum brings you here I'll start worrying.'

'I should be so lucky.'

'Flirt.' She smiled.

'Cynic.'

'Just pull over anywhere,' she instructed. He did, and killed the engine. 'Now, remember, don't let me walk off the cliff or something. I don't come here that often.'

'Jeez, Laney. No pressure.'

It felt good to laugh again after the tension of the past few minutes. 'I just don't want you to forget that you're my Wilbur this afternoon.'

'What happened to wanting equality?'

'I want to live, more.'

She got out as he did, but stayed close to the ute until he came around to her side and placed her hand gently on his bent arm. She took a few tentative steps forward.

'There's a few loose rocks…'

'I'm really only concerned about the big drop that

ends in a splash.' Or a *splat,* probably, if the tide was out. 'The rest is just normal to me.'

He led her forward a short way, then stopped. 'This is about as far as I am comfortable taking you.'

Sweet how nervous he was about this. 'What do you see?'

'More view. More ocean. It's still lovely.'

'Turn around.'

He shuffled them both around so the water was to their back.

'Now what do you see?'

'Wow. *Everything.* It's higher than I realised here. The forest to our left, all green and dense, Mitchell's Cliff in the very far distance, and the highway. Both are Toytown-tiny. And I can even see your homestead and all the honey-harvesting plant in between. Your house looks like it's practically overhanging the ocean from here. No wonder your view is so awesome.'

'Dad says you can see the entirety of the Morgan land from here. That's why he brought Mum here to propose—so she could see what she was getting into the bargain.'

'Did he think she needed a sweetener?'

The truth wasn't quite so romantic. 'No. He wanted her to be clear that she was taking on the life as well as the man. He needed her to know that he wasn't going to change after marriage and that this was where they'd live for ever.'

And their children, and their children's children…

'Did it work?'

'She said that one moment brought it all into crashing focus for her. Morgan's was his life. And so she had to make it hers too. It was all or nothing.'

'But she said yes.'

The tiniest glow filled her, thinking about the love her parents shared. 'Of course. They were perfect for each other.'

'Happily ever after, then?'

'Like all good stories.'

Elliott turned them both back to the ute. 'So, you said something about a basket…?'

'Told you you'd be starving. Even with the honey snack.'

'Stop gloating and start producing.'

Together they unloaded the hastily packed hamper.

Laney turned her back to the stiff breeze coming off the ocean and curled her legs under her. Its every buffet on her back was enhancing her perception of the kind of day it was out on the ocean. Consequently her hair whipped around her face wildly at times.

'You okay there?'

'I figured you might as well get to enjoy the view since it's wasted on me.' Her view was probably of the ute.

'It just got even better, then.'

'Flatterer.' Her laugh was half-snort. 'Totally working, by the way.'

'This is some spread.' He chuckled opposite her. 'Cheese, pickled onions, ham, and more of your mother's bread.'

It occurred to her to tease him for describing for her what was in the picnic that she'd packed herself, but then she realised that the warm sensation under her ribs was because he'd bothered. 'And honey on that bread for dessert.'

'Good choice.'

'Not too rural for you?'

'I had everything but the honey in the gardens of a French church once and called it exotic. I'd be a hypocrite to call it anything else here, with ocean and sky all around us.'

They busied themselves loading ingredients onto thick wedges of bread. Laney had a few moments of self-consciousness, fumbling with the food in front of Elliott, but he didn't comment and he didn't rush in to help her out so she just finished her fumbling and got stuck in to the important job of filling her gnawing stomach.

'So, is your dad still involved with basketball?'

'No idea. I don't know who he is.'

She paused with her sandwich halfway to her mouth. No father and no relationship with his mother. What a lonely childhood. 'Oh…'

His voice shrugged. 'You don't miss what you never had.'

Wasn't that exactly what she'd been trying to tell him about her vision? 'You mean that?'

'When I was little I used to make up complicated fantasies of this famous sportsman coming back for me. Taking me away to be part of his exciting, dynamic life. But the reality is he was just a guy who played basketball well and slept with my mother once. He doesn't even know I exist. But I guess I needed the fantasy to hang on to, so he served his purpose.'

The lie resonated through his thick voice. He cared. He cared a lot.

'Well, that's making *my* dad look pretty golden, hey?' she breathed.

'Your father *is* golden. Astute, driven, family-orientated, committed. What's not to love?'

'I do love him, of course. But I didn't always want to.'

'What do you mean?'

'All that commitment and drive? It can be hard when you're a kid and he's focussing it all on you.'

Fiercely.

All the public services he'd challenged and the concessions he'd pressured the district council into for the only blind person in town. All the letters he'd written. All the calls to his local representative. Making sure that his daughter was not denied one single opportunity in life.

Meaning she'd got a heck of a lot more than the average kid as a result.

'He obviously feels he has a lot to make up to you for.'

'And has done so—many times over. But no kid wants to be the centre of attention like that.'

'Especially not you.'

'Meaning?'

'Meaning I'm starting to understand your reticence to own your achievements.'

'I'm not reluctant, Elliott, I'm just a realist. If I thought for a moment that—'

'Don't move, Laney!'

The urgency in his voice completely stole her attention. Was the cliff-face crumbling? Had a snake appeared from the grass?

'What?'

'Bee.'

The seriousness with which he announced the single word was almost comic. 'Where?'

'On your fringe.'

'Don't kill it.'

He puffed his offence out. 'I'm not going to *kill* it. And—PS—you're hardly in a position to lecture *me* about bee-o-cide.'

She sat, carefully motionless. 'This is a fully grown, fully functioning bee. Where is it now?'

'Just clinging there.'

'It's probably exhausted from fighting the gusts. I'll let it recover out of the wind and then point it towards home.'

She leaned forward slightly and felt her way along the remnants of their meal for the honey. It took two seconds to get a fingertip full of instant bee fuel. 'Left or right?'

'On your left, about five centimetres above your eye.' He *whoah*ed her as she slowly slid her finger up past her ear. 'Right there.'

And then she just…sat there… Feeling absolutely nothing and hearing absolutely nothing except the wind buffeting against her body, but hoping the bee would make its way to the unexpected energy source. Hoping she hadn't disturbed it into flying off, leaving her sitting here looking like a complete idiot.

Though surely he'd tell her.

Surely.

Opening herself up to ridicule was not something that came naturally to her.

'It's feeding.' Amazement saturated Elliott's voice.

She made sure not to move during her little laugh. 'You are *such* a city kid.'

'I'll be sure to return the sentiment when you're in the city and you're experiencing something for the first time.'

Thank goodness for the bee or she'd have jerked her head in his direction—sight or no sight. 'Is that an invitation?'

Silence…

Awkward silence.

'It was an assumption. That you'll be up there one day on business.'

Survival instinct forced her to keep it light. 'Are you tired of country runs already? Wanting us to come to you?'

'Not at all. I enjoy the thinking time on the way down and back. But I guess I can't imagine you *never* visiting the city.' He cleared his throat. 'And

I assumed I'd see you if you did. You know—for lunch or something.'

'Maybe you would. I don't really know anyone else up there.' Why would she? 'So I'd probably have no reason to go.'

'You truly aren't curious at all?'

'Not really. What does the city have that I can't get here? Things that I could enjoy,' she added before he could start peppering her with a long list of things she couldn't see.

'I don't know…elephants?'

The unexpectedness of that stirred a chuckle out of her. 'There are elephants roaming wild in the city?'

'There's a zoo across the river from Ashmore Coolidge's offices full of animals you'd never get down here. And concerts… You could go to a concert.'

'We have one of the state's biggest vineyard concert venues in the next district. They have multiple events every season.'

'You could go to the races…'

'Where do you think all those horses qualify for their city races?'

'Okay, what about the university? You could visit the facial recognition team. I'm sure they'd love to show you their progress in person.'

'Ooh...' That could be quite interesting. *Wait...* When had this stopped being hypothetical and started being something she was actually thinking about? 'Or I could just email them.'

'Just admit it, Laney. You won't know what's interesting until you find yourself being interested by it. Who knows? You might share my passion for parasailing or something equally random.'

She shifted her other hand to support the elbow holding up the finger that was feeding the bee. She wished it would eat faster so she could feel a tiny bit less dopey.

'You parasail?'

'Yeah. I co-own a speedboat with a mate of mine and we go out whenever we can, take turns going up. Why?' His voice grew keen. 'Is that something that interests you?'

If it involved flying, it sure did. 'Maybe.'

'Have you ever done any water sports?'

'Owen taught me to surf a little bit.'

'Were you any good?'

'Not really, but I liked the sensation of just...floating on the swell. Being supported by the waves. I've always wondered if flying would be the same.'

Speaking of flight... In the silence between her words and his answer, she heard the bee give a test buzz of its wings.

'I'll take you parasailing,' he offered.

'Down here?'

'No… On my boat. If we do it then you need to come up to the city.'

Need to. Which meant he wanted her to. 'Why can't you just motor down the coast?'

'I work for Ashmore Coolidge, Laney, not for you. If you want to come out with me on *my* boat on *my* weekend off then you need to come up to *my* turf.'

Firm. Uncompromising. And totally reasonable under the circumstances. Her heart pumped out resentment. She'd fought all her life to get people to treat her like anyone else and now that someone was, was she getting snotty about it? Had she grown up feeling more entitled than she'd realised?

Elliott's challenge hung out there, live and real.

'Okay. Maybe I will,' she said. Never one to back down.

'Good. When?'

Sudden pressure—and something else—fisted in her belly. 'When are you going out next?'

'We were going to try for next weekend. Weather permitting.'

So soon? But she wasn't about to admit how much that freaked her out. 'Okay. Next weekend, then.'

Yikes…

'How about I collect you from the train Saturday morning and drive you back down here Saturday night? Or you could stay over.'

Owen had once described the flashing lights of an ambulance that had passed and she saw them now, vivid in her imagination. She definitely heard them.

Or you could stay over.

You know, just like that…

She ignored that part of his comment completely. Very grown-up of her. 'I'm sure you've got better things to do with your Saturday night than chauffeur me around.'

'Not really. Plus then I can finish up my review of your facilities and we'll have something to decide.'

'Um…okay, then?'

'Is that a question or a statement?'

What was she doing? She was twenty-five years old, for crying out loud. Why was she letting him get to her like this? She wanted to flick her hair back defiantly but didn't out of respect for the bee. Instead she just sat up straighter.

'It's a statement. Yes. I'll take the train up next Saturday.'

'Great. I'll schedule it in.'

Elliott's carefully moderated tone was pretty slick, but she'd been mining people's voices for subtext her whole life. She could hear enthusiasm under all the nonchalance. The question was, was he pleased she was coming out on his boat next week or was he just pleased he'd got his way?

Yeah, well, good luck with that. Hopefully, his super corporate training had prepared him for disappointment. Because squiring her around the city wasn't going to change her mind one bit about taking Morgan's global.

The tiny buzz past her ear was her only evidence that the bee had finished its pitstop and headed off back towards its hive.

'At last!' she groaned, lowering her aching arm and slipping her still honeyed finger between her lips.

'You have honey in your hair.'

And before she could do much more than wince about how undignified that particular image was the slight rattle of the food containers on the picnic blanket told her that Elliott had braced a hand amongst them so that his other hand could brush against her forehead gently, plucking the offending lock away from her skin.

He lingered in that position, his knuckles gently brushing against her forehead. 'Want me to pour some water on it?'

'No. I'll have a shower when we get home. Wash it out.'

Obviously. Heck—you'd think she'd never been touched by a man before.

A few slight tugs on her hair told her he was removing the worst of it, but then he let his knuckles brush the rest of her hair back away from her face.

'Your eyes look very blue up here,' he murmured. All close and breathy.

All the better not to see you with. 'What do they usually look like?'

'Grey. Bottomless.'

Even shrugging felt almost beyond her as his knuckles curled and turned into fingers instead. Blue, grey... It was meaningless at the best of times, and this definitely wasn't her brain at its best. It was completely fixated on Elliott's fingers as they brushed—as light and soft as they had been for such a short moment the first time he'd come here—down her jaw.

'Stay still...'

He took her clean fingers in his, raised them to his face, and placed them gently on his own cheek.

'Knock yourself out,' he breathed. Low, intimate. Just a hint of gravel.

Every part of her tightened up. She didn't move her hand a single millimetre. But she didn't take it off, either.

'When I said learning someone's face was something very personal I didn't mean just for you.'

'I know. But I'm hoping since I just played with your hair I've broken the ice sufficiently.'

'Sufficiently for what?'

'That you might be comfortable enough, now, to let your fingers see what I look like.'

'Why?'

'Because I'd like you to know.'

'Why?'

His puff of breath tickled her wrist. 'I have no idea.'

The raw, confused honesty of that disarmed her enough to spread the fingers of her right hand slightly and spider them gently up his face. The rasp of a half-day's stubble teased her sensitive pads and resonated deep down inside her. Incentive enough to move away from the strong angles of his jawline across towards his nose. She kept her trajectory upward so that she bypassed his lips.

Pure survival instinct.

Nose: pretty much where you'd expect to find it, and with the slight kink he'd told her about. Strong wide brow with eyebrows a heck of a lot tamer than her father's.

'Did you cut your hair?'

'No. Why?'

'You said your hair fell down over your brow.'

His fingers came up to guide hers further upward, to where his hair sat neatly corralled against the buffeting winds.

'Is that…?' She frowned at the very thought. 'Is that bee wax?'

'It's a hard styling wax. Commercial.'

She hadn't pegged him for a manscaper. 'Styling wax doesn't get any manlier just because you put the word "hard" in front of it.'

'Surely Owen and his mates use product in their hair before a big night out?'

Her fingers paused on his forehead and she wondered that he'd consider a few hours with her on the farm as worthy of grooming. 'We'd be lucky if they *combed* their hair before a big night out.'

'Why are you frowning?'

'Just thinking of a potential market. Hair wax.'

The shift of facial muscles under her fingers suggested he was smiling, but his voice confirmed it. 'Can't keep a good businesswoman down.'

She raised her other hand and put both sets of fingers to work exploring the texture of his hair, rubbing the waxy residue between her thumb and forefinger. Getting a sense of it.

'Interesting.'

'My hair or my face?'

Right. His face… That was what she was sup-posed to be doing. Not playing with his thick hair.

She fluttered her right hand back down past his eye and along his cheekbone, and then—when she couldn't delay the moment of truth a moment lon-ger—quickly traced her middle fingers across his *'I'm told I have kissable'* lips. They parted just slightly before she could leave them and breath heated her finger-pads for half a heartbeat.

'So there you go,' Elliott rumbled, then cleared his throat. 'Now you've really seen me.'

A nervous smile broke free. 'And played with your hair for longer than is polite. Though what do you mean, *really* seen you?'

'You know how I sound, how I smell and how I feel. That's pretty much all your available senses taken care of.'

'Well,' she began, 'I haven't—'

Stop!

At the very, *very* last moment her brain kicked into gear and slammed her throat shut on what had been about to come tumbling out.

I haven't tasted you yet.

She was thinking about her four senses. That was all. But there was no way she could even joke about it without it sounding like the lamest come-on ever. Not after she'd just had her fingers in his hair, all over his mouth. Not after she'd spent a relaxed afternoon testing out the waters of flirtation and had had the honey equivalent of foreplay down in the extraction sheds.

'You haven't what?'

His voice, his breath, seemed impossibly closer, yet he hadn't moved the rest of his body one inch.

'Nothing. Never mind.'

'Were you going to say *tasted*?'

'No.' The denial sounded false even to her. And it came way too fast.

'Really?' His soft voice was full of smile. 'Because it sounded like you were.'

'No. That would be an inappropriate comment to make in the workplace.'

Yes. Work. Good.

'Luckily, we're on our lunch break.'

She clung to her only salvation. 'It's still inappropriate.'

'I agree,' Elliott murmured. 'Then again, that ship sailed when I asked you to touch my face, so what else do I have to lose?'

Her brain was dallying dangerously over his 'touch my face' and so it missed the meaning in his words until it was too late.

His lips—the ones she'd gone to so much trouble to avoid touching—pressed lightly onto Laney's—

half open, soft and damp and warm—before mould-
ing more snugly against her. Sealing up the gaps. It
took her a moment to acclimatise to the feeling of
someone else's breath on her lips and he took full
advantage of her frozen surprise to open further
and gently swipe the tip of his tongue over her hyper-sensitive and suddenly oxygen-deprived lips.

Elliott Garvey was *kissing* her.

Not that it was her first kiss, but it had certainly
been long enough between drinks that she'd virtually forgotten what it felt like to have a man's mouth
on hers. How it felt and how it smelled and—her
whole body just about melted—how he *tasted.* Her
senses were flooded with the lime spritzer they'd
just been drinking, and fine cheese, and a whole
under-palate of *oh, my freaking goodness!*

Elliott Garvey was kissing *her.*

Instinct made her stretch her neck to fit against
him better just as he might have pulled back—before she could think better of it, before she could
let him go. She lapped at the heavy weight of his
bottom lip, adding her breath to his and letting her
tongue slip against his teeth. His hand speared in
amongst her thick hair and curled warm and strong
around her skull.

They tangled like that for moments—exploring,
testing—his tongue gently asking and hers honestly

answering. Sighing against the smoothness of his hot flesh. Deciding it wasn't enough.

Elliott pulled back the moment she opened to him, his voice thick-breathed and guttural on her name. Cool coastal air rushed into the vacuum caused by his rapidly withdrawn kiss.

'Your eyes are closed,' he breathed.

Another instinctive adaptation, apparently, because she hadn't meant to close them. She concentrated on opening them now. And on staring exactly where his should be as if that would help her somehow read his expression—to back up the Morse code of his rapid thumb-pulse against her scalp— so she could know what he was thinking. Whether stopping was what he'd wanted to do. Whether he'd been as engaged and excited by that kiss as she had.

Whether she'd just made a massive arse of herself.

'Wow.' Not only could she not trust herself to say more, she had no idea in the world what the right thing to say was.

But it seemed he did. 'Laney, I'm sorry.'

The cool rush of air was suddenly a bucket of cold salty water. 'For kissing me?'

'I didn't mean for it to go that far.'

Okay... 'How far did you mean it to go?' And exactly how much thought had he given it?

Breath hissed out of him and he moved further

back still. 'Not that far. I was curious. I'd been wanting to do that all day. And I shouldn't have.'

'Why not?'

'Because you're *you*, Laney.'

Confusion stabbed fast and low in her belly. 'Because I'm a client? Because I'm blind?'

'Because you don't kiss strange men every other day.'

Well, that was as good as a slap across the face. Was her limited experience so very tangible? She'd been completely lost in *his* kiss. 'Whereas you kiss strange women regularly?'

'Yeah, actually. If you really want me to answer that.'

No, thanks.

'You're not a stranger.'

'I'm not far off it.'

'*You* kissed *me*,' she pointed out, and then cringed at the defensive edge to her words.

His voice gentled. 'I'm not sorry I kissed you, Laney. I'm just sorry it got as heavy as it did so fast.'

Surely that was like expecting the ocean to apologise for eroding the bluff. 'Oh, really? What *is* the right time to get hot and heavy, in your vast experience?'

'After one date, at least.'

It burned her that his voice could be tinged with humour. She guessed he *was* more used to casual kissing than she was. He sure recovered faster.

'You have a very robust ego if you think I'm going to be going on a date with you.'

'You have to. You promised.'

'Parasailing is not a date. It's a...' What was it, exactly? It was a man asking a woman to go out on his boat. Known in normal circles as *a date*.

If an eyebrow lifting could make a sound, Elliott's somehow made it. She could *see* his twitch as clearly as if her eyes worked. That was how tangible his arrogance was.

Her chin lifted. 'It's an arrangement.'

'Right—okay, then.'

'So there will be no kissing after it.'

'Understood.'

'Just like there shouldn't have been any today.'

'I concur.'

She sat back more fully on her haunches and that was when she realised exactly how far forward she'd leaned to half-consume his tongue. Mortified heat flushed in a hot wave up her neck.

'Right, then.' But the hint of a sound drifted over the ocean to her ears. 'Are you...*laughing*?'

'Of course I'm laughing. This is crazy.'

'Why is it crazy?'

'Because *of course* parasailing is a date, and *of course* I'm going to kiss you afterwards. I just wanted to give you some time to get used to the idea instead of mauling you when you can't run away without plunging to your death.'

A totally foreign kind of light-headedness washed over her. How bad could she have been if he wanted to kiss her again? And how was she going to endure seven days before it happened, now that she knew how good he tasted.

'I didn't kiss you because I felt obligated, Elliott,' she confessed. 'I really wanted to know what it would be like.'

'My robust ego is very happy to hear it.'

And then there didn't seem much more to be said about it. Elliott Garvey wasn't like those other men—man-boys, really—that she'd dated. He wasn't pitying her or objectifying her or out for any kind of social kudos. He just wanted to kiss her.

Simple as that.

'You're smiling.'

Yeah, she was. She was happy. But she wasn't about to let him know that. 'It's an awkward smile. I don't know what to do now.'

'You don't have to do anything. Just enjoy the sun.'

Really? The sun was shining? Impossible to see

it past the honking great *glow* that was Elliott in her awareness. He pulsed, thick and strong, right at the front of her brain.

Silence descended—as uncomfortable and un-ignorable as Elliott seemed to think it *wasn't*.

Until he broke it.

'More cheese?'

Stupid how he busied himself refilling her plate to disguise the tremor in hands Laney couldn't even see, but the simple chore helped him to focus and regroup. That and a decent whack of deep breathing.

Kissing had not been on his radar for this afternoon, though the residual tension in his body following the honey-sucking incident was very happy that it had eventuated. The only thing he'd been expecting—planning—was to get to know Laney better. To address some question marks. He just hadn't realised that *What does she taste like?* was one of his questions.

Though now that he had an answer he could see how very clearly it had been. Since the whole dancing on the beach thing, if he was honest.

He blew out a silent fortifying breath.

He'd had to use all his corporate skills to gather

his scattered wits and reassemble them so that he could speak with even the slightest wit after his lips had touched hers. He'd kissed a lot of women—countless—but they didn't usually render him mute the way her soft, tentative exploration had.

Maybe that was it. Maybe he was just used to kisses being more forthright. Kisses usually came sure and easy, because he gravitated towards women who were guaranteed to be interested. Women who were into money. Women who were into him.

Who knew that all this time he should have been kissing women who *weren't* into him?

Though the idea that Laney Morgan might not be into him bordered on the edge of alarming. Which was disturbing in itself.

And he didn't *do* disturbing. No more than he did *need*. In fact he didn't do anything in which the outcome wasn't reasonably assured. Even in business he did his due diligence and only went after the sure-thing clients. Life was just safer that way.

He'd assumed a small outfit like Morgan's would jump at the chance for some guided development into the global sphere, and he didn't understand Laney's reticence any more than he understood what she did to him.

Correction: he understood very well *what* she

did to him, but he didn't understand why. Or how. She wasn't even trying. Yet with no apparent effort on her part she'd captivated him as surely as any of the bees in her hives. They thought they were free to come and go, too. But they weren't—not really.

It was kind of insidious now that he thought about it.

Still…knowledge was power. There was no reason he shouldn't continue to explore whatever this was between them now that he knew how Laney worked. And how well *innocent* and *passionate* worked on *him*, particularly.

Two things he hadn't been for a really long time. If he ever had.

He tried to trace the emptiness inside him back to a time when it had never existed but failed. It was something he'd carried around with him always. When he was younger he'd used it to keep all his adolescent angst in, then later he filled it with his relentless globetrotting adventures, and now it was a handy repository for all his corporate ambition.

He'd once been stupid enough to do his own packing when moving apartment, and he knew exactly how many newspapers he'd balled up to pack into the empty spaces around his many belongings.

They did the job, but ultimately they ended up in the recycling.

Laney was just balled newspaper. This fascination he had for her—the fullness he felt when he was with her—it was all just incredibly attractive, stimulating, emotional stuffing. It took the edge off the gnawing hollow, but it wouldn't take much to send it tumbling back out onto the floor.

It wouldn't last. Nothing ever did, in his experience. The one favour his mother had done for him was to instil in him, early on, an acceptance of the disappointments of life. It took a lot to crush him these days, because he didn't let himself count on anything.

Or anyone.

The void was so much a part of him it was impossible to imagine being the man he was without it. Or to imagine what other people kept in theirs. It was tempting to ask Laney, because surely the most fulfilled woman he'd ever known would have to have the answer.

Or maybe he could mine the answer for himself if he just spent more time with her. Really got under her skin.

His whole body high-fived that notion. Even if it was ultimately doomed.

Even if it did nothing more than highlight how big his void had become while he was ignoring it.

Really, what were the chances he *wouldn't* support any plan that ended in him spending more time with Laney Morgan?

CHAPTER SEVEN

LUCKY SHE WAS a country girl, so being dropped at Mitchell's Cliff train station at five a.m. by her father hadn't felt too unusual. Well, the time hadn't felt odd. Being on a train alone for the first time ever kind of did, but she hunkered down in her comfortable seat, squeezed her earbuds in and cranked up her audiobook for the ninety-minute journey north to the big smoke, doing her best not to think about how out of her comfort zone she was.

Alone on a train without Wilbur, whose last city-guiding experience had been thirteen years ago.

But wasn't that the point? Parasailing wasn't exactly in her comfort zone either, but she was super-keen to try that. So why would being on a train freak her out? All around her passengers commuted to the city—some every morning and evening for work—and they managed.

So would she.

She had her stick. She'd be fine.

Yet as she rested her hand lightly on the forearm

of the train security guard ninety minutes later, as he led her towards the exit, she was super-glad that Elliott would be meeting her on the platform. Because although she knew that she would be able to ask her way to the taxi rank and a driver who would get her easily to Elliott's house, there was something extra comforting about knowing he'd be waiting right there for her.

Comforting and welcoming.

And not just because he was Elliott.

'Uneventful journey, Laney?'

His deep voice sounded from directly behind her as the security guard released her on the city platform. Her small thanks were totally lost in the ambient noise on the platform, much higher than she was used to, and all the different smells practically assaulting her nostrils with their diversity. Even the underfoot vibrations caused by so many trains coming in and out of the station made her feel less certain of any step she took.

It made her wonder what city folk *did* with all that sensory input.

She was too rattled by the unfamiliarity of the journey and the stimulus here in the station to remember to be rattled by *him*. By what they'd shared just a few short days ago. Or by what he'd effectively promised they would share again today.

That was something to worry about when they got somewhere quiet.

'Elliott. Hi.'

It took him just moments to guide her out of the station to his waiting car, and she broke her own rule by gripping his forearm rather than just resting her own on top of it.

This was a grippy kind of day.

At last she sank into the luxurious comfort of deep leather seats and the expensive seals on the door blocked out the city.

She turned to him and breathed out her relief on an extended greeting—another one—flexing the kinks out of her fingers. Okay, so maybe her grip *was* a bit tight.

'You okay?' Elliott asked.

'New places are always that bit more stressful. I'll be fine now that I'm here.' She fought her subconscious' great desire to say *with you*.

'Have you had breakfast?'

No. Because she'd been too nervous. 'Just coffee.'

'That might work for you in the country, but here a coffee doesn't fuel you until morning tea. Not with what we'll be doing today.'

She was as intrigued by the idea of a day full of activity as she was by the fact he'd remembered her words, almost verbatim, from a full week ago.

'You're going to be towing me behind your speed-boat. I don't want to revisit that breakfast at an inopportune moment.'

His chuckle blended perfectly with the purr that was his car ignition. 'We're not going out for a few hours. You'll have plenty of time to digest.'

She'd forgotten that it was not yet seven a.m. 'What will we do until then?'

'I had a chat with the team from VisApis. They're in their lab today and have offered to show us around at nine. So we've got time for something a bit more substantial than just coffee.'

The queasy void in her belly was rapidly closing over just at being back in the familiar warmth of Elliott's company. The glow was fully back in residence, too, and this time it had brought its good friend, tingles. They skittered up and down her limbs.

'Okay. I could definitely eat.'

But just because she *could* eat a full country breakfast didn't mean she wanted to. She still had the niggling concern that she might not take to flight quite as naturally as she secretly dreamed. But organic muesli wasn't too much of a risk and was pretty quickly digested. And she only had a small portion. Elliott had himself a poached egg on a bagel and a gorgeous-smelling coffee, which meant they were easily done in time to drive over to the university and meet with the VisApis crew by nine.

Elliott gave her mother a run for her money as chief scene-setter, describing everything as he drove along the foreshore of the city and followed the river around to one of the established leafy suburbs to its west. Laney was fascinated by his mixed descriptions of the architecture in the suburb, or the odd statues mounted out in the river itself, the portly pelicans roosting on posts along the way, until finally they pulled up at the base of one of the old limestone campus buildings he'd been describing.

'Okay, here we are.'

VisApis's research labs. The place where the studies they undertook at Morgan's had triggered more study on the ability of bees to map the features of human faces.

'The theory is that they use the same ability they use on flowers to discriminate between human faces,' she continued on as Elliott helped her out of his car..

'And you're a favoured flower?'

'They clearly appreciate my extra-gentle handling.'

'So you're in on the ground level with a poten-
tially lucrative discovery?'

She shrugged. 'I just wanted to understand more
about the bees.'

'And Edison just wanted to know how to make a
lightbulb last longer,' Elliott said, guiding her up a
short staircase. 'All innovation begins with a simple question.'

'You're not suggesting the two are even remotely
on the same scale?'

'I guess it depends what it leads to in the future.
VisApis are claiming their work will revolutionise
facial recognition.'

'*Their* work…' she reinforced. 'I'm sure they were
glad for the lead study, but I can't imagine they've
spared much of a thought for me or the original
bunch of bees since.'

'That's why they jumped at the chance to meet
you today.'

She hadn't thought about how he might have
asked. 'Oh, I hope this isn't awkward,' she said.

'Only one way to find out.'

Ordinarily Elliott wouldn't get quite so hands-on
with a client—a woman—but Laney's lack of sight
gave him the perfect excuse to touch her. He rested
his hand at her lower back and kept the contact up

as she negotiated the entry to the building with her cane. It was a greedy pleasure that he felt vaguely ashamed of.

A research assistant greeted them with a smile just inside the entrance.

'Ms Morgan,' the young man practically gushed. 'It's a real pleasure.'

Two extra lines appeared between Laney's brows, but she didn't voice whatever question she'd developed, instead smiling at the man and turning in the direction of his voice to follow him down the hall. Elliott stepped up close behind her so she knew he was still there.

It only took him a few minutes in the lab to understand the reverence, though.

Everywhere he looked computers belonging to the personnel who weren't at work on a Saturday flashed a single word and logo in syncopated order across their dormant screensavers—HELENA. The six letters were stylishly designed along with a close-up illustrated version of one of her eyes. He'd know that grey anywhere.

They'd named their software after her.

'Ms Morgan—at last.' A more senior man in a crisp lab coat introduced himself to her as the project leader.

Laney's soft hair shifted with the tilt of her head. 'Are we late?'

'I'm sorry, no.' The man's laugh boomed. 'I meant it's a pleasure to meet you after all this time. Those of us who have been working on Helena for two years wondered if we'd ever get the pleasure.'

Elliott held his breath. This could end badly.

'You...' Her frown was very definitely real this time. 'You named your project after me?'

Another thing he really liked about her. She didn't waste anyone's time with fake humility.

'To the rest of the world this project is VisApis 439, but we know it affectionately as Helena. And, yes, we named it for you, since it was born out of the research you commissioned.'

Standing this close behind her, Elliott knew the moment she stiffened like an old lock.

'Morgan's commissioned it.'

'But it was *your* experiences that led us to the software breakthrough we'd been chasing for a decade. If not for your experiences we never would have looked at bees.'

For the first and only time he was grateful for Laney's lack of sight. Lord only knew what she'd make of her name splashed across their whole lab. Affectionate or otherwise... And then as he looked around the lab he saw all the evidence of how they'd planned for her visit.

Every chair was pushed in at every computer terminal, every bin had been lifted onto the empty desktops. Every obstacle had been kindly and carefully cleared.

'We're looking forward to learning more about your project,' Elliott broke in, intentionally leaning on the word 'your'. He wanted today to go well—all of it—and this fawning over Laney wasn't the fastest path there.

Fortunately the guy wasn't just engineer-smart. He picked up on Elliott's subtle cue and moved smoothly on to a civilian version of how the software worked and what they were already able to do with it. Elliott used the time well to surreptitiously pull out a chair or two specifically for Laney to negotiate. She did her part by nudging them with her cane and neatly sidestepping them.

It was nearly ninety minutes before they'd seen all the progress the team had made and Laney had answered the many questions the project director had about her observations on bees—and he hers—but finally Elliott gave her his arm to manage the exit.

'I liked them,' she announced, halfway down the steps.

'I'd say the feeling was mutual.'

'They didn't Laney-proof their entire office.'

Any residual guilt he'd felt at littering the office with obstacles evaporated. 'That's important to you?'

'I hate being catered for. I don't expect it and I don't enjoy it.'

Something she'd said once before echoed again. That her father had pushed constantly for others to make allowances for his little girl.

'I like that my sight is the least interesting part of the process for them.'

Two thoughts collided then. First that their choice of name for the software suggested that wasn't at all true, and second—strong and dominant—that he didn't want Laney heaping gratitude on any man other than him.

A nicely prehistoric little sentiment.

He'd been going out of his way to treat her just like anyone else. He'd been suppressing his own masculine instincts to rescue her every five minutes. It rankled that the white coats had earned her respect so easily—and so quickly—when she seemed to give respect away so sparingly.

Right behind that he realised how important her good opinion was to him.

And right behind *that* he realised that he was still sixteen emotionally.

Come on, Garvey. Man up.

He forced the conversation back on track. 'What did you think of their progress?'

'I think it's exciting. And amazing. I look forward to when it's finished.'

'How do you feel about them naming it after you?'

'Their choice, I guess.'

'It's not an honour?'

'It'll be good for Morgan's to be associated with the research,' she hedged.

Morgan's again. Never Laney. A big part of him wanted her to know that was *her name* emblazoned across their lab. Hers, not her family's. But that wouldn't be helpful to his cause.

'Well, thanks for indulging the detour,' he said, settling her back into the passenger seat. 'It really helped me to understand the project. And the potential.'

'I'd have thought this sort of thing was too random to reliably count as potential.'

'The specifics, maybe. But research could be a good sideline for Morgan's. You can only accommodate so many bees in labs, and Morgan's can offer researchers the kind of sample sizes they need to get verifiable results. Tens of thousands. Maybe there are other partnerships like this one you can form in the future.'

Tiny creases appeared between her brows.

'That worries you?'

'I just like the…the organic nature of our business. No pun intended.'

'You get less joy out of things that are planned?'

'Maybe.'

'Are you looking forward to today?'

Her head turned to him, though it didn't need to. 'Parasailing? Yes, very much.'

'We planned that.'

'Yeah, but can you imagine how much more exciting it would have been if you'd said to me up at the bluff, "*Come on, Laney, whack on this harness. We're jumping from the cliff right now*".'

'But then you'd miss out on all the anticipation. The build-up.'

'Build-up matters?'

'Laney… Build-up is the best bit.' His car purred to life at the press of a button. 'Didn't you have to plan things out growing up?'

She didn't answer and a lightbulb flashed on above his head, bright and obvious.

That's exactly why she prefers spontaneity, moron.

He paused just before clicking his seatbelt into

place and leaned over her before he thought better of it. She stiffened slightly with surprise, but didn't push him away when he brushed his lips over hers.

'What was that for?'

The warm caress of her breath on his lips teased them to life even more. 'I was being spontaneous.'

'By kissing me?'

'You were probably expecting it at the end of the day.'

'I wasn't— I'm not *expecting* anything.'

But that wasn't anger flushing red over her shirt collar. She liked it. Either the kiss or the exhilaration. Didn't much matter which. He was just pleased to have finally unravelled a bit more of the mysterious Ms Morgan.

'Well, you can expect an awesome afternoon on the water. Next stop the Indian Ocean.'

CHAPTER EIGHT

'SERIOUSLY, DUDE. A blind chick?'

Elliott threw Danny his most withering stare. 'She's not a "chick", Dan. She's a woman.'

Danny flicked his gaze to where Laney sat, firm-knuckled around *Misfit*'s gunnel, her white shirt blown back tight against her torso. Showcasing every curve. Elliott instantly felt protective of those curves, because she couldn't see them to know how uncovered they were by either her one-piece swim-suit or the translucent shirt. It felt vaguely wrong to be appreciating them.

'She sure is.' Danny grinned. 'A *blind* woman.'

'So?'

'So that's not your usual type.'

'That's the least of the ways Helena Morgan is not my type, Danny.' He kept his voice low, just in case the laws of physics suddenly decided to change direction and carry their words to her extra-percep-tive ears. 'What's your point?'

'My point is what are you doing? Is this serious? Is it casual? Is it work?'

'What does it matter?'

'It matters, mate. If this is work then why is she here, out riding with us? And if this is casual then you might have picked the wrong girl to hit.'

'She's blind, Dan, not impaired.' The vehemence of his own voice surprised him. 'She's as capable as any other woman of dealing with something short term.'

'And that's what this is? A bit of short-term something?'

No. It wasn't as seedy as Danny made it sound. He'd thought he knew, but he was starting to doubt his own mind. 'It's not anything.'

Yet—and only if you didn't count two kisses and the impending promise of more.

'I wanted to get her off the farm. Have a chance to talk with her in a different context.'

Danny glanced back at him from the wheel of *Misfit*. 'Why?'

Good question. 'To see what makes her tick.'

'Why do you need to know that?'

You didn't buy a boat with someone if they weren't a good mate, but that wasn't something he was prepared to answer honestly to himself, let alone his best friend. 'Because this job hangs on getting her co-operation.'

Ugh, when had he become such a good liar?

'Ah, so it *is* work. Are Ashmore Coolidge cool with you sleeping with your clients?'

'I'm not sleeping with her. And the firm trusts me to use my best judgement.'

'In other words they're cool with you sleeping with a client if it leads to revenue?'

'I'm *not* sleeping with her.'

'Right.'

'Damn it, Danny—'

'Hey, I'm just trying to work out if I should bother getting to know her.'

'She wants to try parasailing. That's it.'

'Mmm.'

'Mmm, what?'

'Smacks of dirty pool, Elliott. Getting her high on adrenaline and then hitting her up for whatever it is you want.'

Anger bubbled hard and fast just below the place where he usually kept it contained. 'That's not what I'm doing. She just wants to experience something new.'

Though wasn't he? Could he truly say it hadn't crossed his mind how good a kiss between them would be right after she landed? Or in the air?

Danny eyeballed him. 'And since when did you become a life coach?'

'Why are you busting my brass about this?'

'There's a blind woman clinging to the front of our boat. That's not usual, man.'

Elliott's eyes narrowed and focussed on Laney's white-knuckled grip on the chrome catch bars that lined the bow. Was that just a secure farm grip… or was she absolutely terrified?

Danny must have read his mind. 'Is she okay out there?'

'She's fine.'

'What if she falls off?'

Irritation warred with concern. 'Last time I checked, blindness didn't affect grip.'

'But what if she does?'

'Then she treads water until we circle back and pick her up, like anyone else.'

His friend gaped at him. 'That's harsh, man.'

'She *can't see*, Danny. She's not a two-year-old.'

In one *whump* it all hit him—how tired Laney must be of being treated as if she was a child. Or disabled. When she was the least disabled disabled person he'd ever met. How the two sides of her must come into conflict all the time—the independent woman who didn't want to be treated with kid gloves and the gentle soul who appreciated that everyone truly meant well.

Danny meant well and Elliott wanted to thump him already. 'Just treat her like anyone else. Except maybe ease up on the ogling.'

'She can't see me do it.'

'No, but I can.'

With that, he swung around the boat's windshield and manoeuvred his way up to the bow to join Laney. Despite the strong headwinds caused by their speed she either heard his approach or felt his footfalls, because her head tilted towards him just slightly even as her hands tightened even more.

He raised his voice over *Misfit*'s motor. 'Okay, Laney?'

'Loving it.' The wind almost stole her words from him.

He shuffled closer. 'Your knuckles are looking a little pale…'

'I didn't say I wasn't also terrified.'

He slid down next to her and matched her death-grip on the chrome trip rail.

'I think this is the fastest I've ever gone in my life.'

'Really? I thought for sure Owen would have put the pedal to the metal a time or two out on the back roads.'

'Yeah, he has. But I didn't have my head out of the window like Wilbur so it's not the same. And although I've doubled with someone on a horse once it was a shire horse, to take our combined weights, so it didn't get up a whole lot of speed.'

'Want us to slow down?'

'No! This is awesome.'

But her knuckles weren't getting any pinker, and again he realised how many things she must have done in her life *despite* her fear. And right behind that he realised that she wouldn't necessarily have been any more or less afraid even if she could see the water whizzing by at one hundred and thirty kilometres per hour.

She tipped her head back and opened her mouth. 'I love the spray.'

The salt and the speed.

'It stings.'

'*Pfff.* This is nothing.'

Her bees. He chuckled, then raised his voice to be heard. 'No. I guess not.'

'So where are we going in such a hurry?'

'There's a sandbar east of here. We use that as a launch site.'

'You don't lift off from the boat?'

'Not if we have a choice. And not when we're doing tandem. It's easier from terra firma.'

That brought her head around again. 'We're going up together?'

'You think I'm going to send you up alone on your first flight?'

What kind of a man did she think he was?

'Can it hold two?'

His laugh barked out of him. 'We'll find out.'

But she wasn't laughing.

'Yes, Laney. It can hold two. And this isn't optional. You've never parasailed before.'

Her frown didn't ease.

'Who did you think was going to give you instructions?'

'I didn't really think about that. In my head it's all very…'

'Organic?'

'Something like that.'

Misfit lost speed. 'Well, you're about to find out. The sandbar is just ahead of us.'

'When you feel my body move, just move with it. Like we're dancing.'

No. If they were dancing she'd be facing him, respectably, instead of strapped in tight with her back to his big, hard chest. Like upright spooning.

'And as soon as you feel the upward tug if you

don't think you can run with me then just lift your legs.'

'And let you do all the work?'

'The boat is doing all the work, really. I'm just keeping us upright.'

Yeah. That was all he was doing. He wasn't giving her the experience of her life. He wasn't keeping her thundering heartbeat in check by his very presence.

He took her again through the basic instructions and then treble-checked the harnesses. Every yank nudged her body closer to his; every buckle-rattle brushed her body with his knuckles. In case she'd forgotten how close together they were standing.

His friend gently revved the boat a way off the sandbar.

'Ready, Laney? Bend forward.'

Right. Because that wasn't suggestive *at all* when you were tucked this close to a man.

But she had no choice as his chest and shoulders bent towards her—

'Now, *run!*'

She did—absolutely determined not to pike out and lift her legs. It took a certain amount of trust to run on unfamiliar terrain, but being strapped to Elliott went a long way to reassuring her that he'd have checked their path for obstacles if for no other reason than his own preservation. His feet ploughed into the sand next to hers—virtually between hers—until the promised yank came, and then another closely after it, and suddenly there was no more sand to plunge her feet into and the harness pulled up taut between her thighs.

And she was running on thin air.

Her stomach didn't lurch, as she'd half expected, and the only clue that they were ascending was the circulation-restricting pressure of the harness and the gentle whoosh of air diagonally down her face.

'Danny's turned on the winch,' he said, and sure enough, the sounds around them changed as they lifted further and further from the ocean. Less boat, more sky.

'How far up will we go?'

'We have two hundred and fifty metres on the winch.'

She knew which hives were a quarter of a kilometre from the house and tried to imagine that in an upward direction. It was tough imagining *high* when you'd never seen it. Or felt it, particularly.

They fell to silence and before too long that was more or less what they had. Even the rumbly engine of *Misfit* and the sounds of the sea were replaced with the sounds of...

'Nothing,' she murmured.

'What?' Elliott leaned in closer to her ear and the comparative warmth of his breath on her cheek was the first time she'd noticed that her skin was so cool. Even though it was a warm autumn day.

'I wasn't expecting it to be so quiet,' she said, and barely needed to raise her voice. 'I thought there'd be whooshing.'

'Danny's slowed the boat to a gentle run.'

'Can you describe what you see?'

He could. He did a great job—not quite as good as her talented mother, but not bad for a rookie, and better again than his descriptions of buildings. He talked about the shape of the land, the winding line of the coast. The island off in the distance to their left. Her brain immediately adjusted and added her version of an island to her imagined vista and she nestled into the deepness of his voice.

The cold nip of the air, the complete ambient silence, the amplified sense of altitude that his words had given her—they all had an effect. She swallowed back the emotion.

'Even the gulls are below us. We're up with the tradewinds. I'll let you know if I see an albatross.'

For some reason the very idea of that hit a place deep down inside her where she'd never looked—a place of longing and loss and what would never be—and tears began to trickle from her eyes. She would never see an albatross hanging on the current. And she sure as heck wouldn't hear it or touch it, so, for her, albatrosses might as well not exist.

'Laney, are you crying?'

'No,' she croaked through thickening tears.

He leaned forward and around as best he could to look at her. 'Don't cry.'

All that did was open the floodgates.

'It's not crying,' she sobbed—though what exactly *was* it? 'It's appreciation. Thank you, Elliott. I might never have had a chance to do this.'

Just above her head he shuffled something and freed up one gloved hand. He used it to stroke some loose damp hair away from her face. 'You're welcome. Just enjoy the view.'

He said that as if he meant every word, and she wondered if he finally *understood* how she worked. Because she *did* have a view—just as real as his. She just didn't see it the way he did.

Their flight—their silence—seemed to go on for eternity. Laney took to wiggling her toes against the cold, and to make sure she had some circulation still happening in legs compromised by the tightness of the harness. She was going to have to run again when they landed, and she didn't want to be the one to send them both plunging face-first into the sandbar.

'So…' he started, still so close behind her. 'How are you feeling about the prospect of more between Morgan's and Ashmore Coolidge?'

'Really? You want to talk about that *now*?'

'Well, we're up here for a while. You want to talk about that kiss instead?'

Ah…no. Not while she was pressed this close to him. She was likely to tip her head back and go for a repeat performance.

'I'm not sure my feelings about growth have changed at all.'

'You still don't trust me?'

His voice was like one of her favourite wines. Full-bodied with things unsaid, but carrying undertones of something more subtle—defensiveness, hurt.

'It's not a question of trust. It's a question of need. I was honest with you when I said I didn't see a need for Morgan's to grow. Why would that have changed just because I've shown you a few things?'

'The research?'

'I can see merit in that but I don't think giving access to a few researchers is the level of growth Ashmore Coolidge is thinking of, somehow.'

'No. You're right. We have our sights set much higher.'

And by 'we' he meant 'he'.

'I don't want you to be disappointed, Elliott. That you've wasted so much time.'

'It's not a waste, Laney. I've met you.'

Her heart lurched, but it was easy to blame it on the sudden dip of the parachute. Far below Danny must have given *Misfit* a burst of speed, because they lifted again almost immediately.

'And I've met your parents and completed Morgan's biennial health check.'

Of course. 'Did we pass?'

'What do you think?'

'I think that means you've seen everything we needed to show you.'

I think that means it's time for you to go.

But Elliott going was not something Laney was prepared to acknowledge just now. 'Well, then, that's a conversation for tomorrow. Between all of us.'

Because she was no more willing to speak for Morgan's than she was to accept praise for all of its achievements. Morgan's was a family brand and this would be a family decision.

'Does that mean you're staying in the city tonight? I got the spare room ready in case.'

'I think that would be hard to explain to my parents.' *Oh, you coward.* 'But I thought…to save you driving back down on Sunday…'

'You want me to stay over on the farm tonight?'

His question—practically pressed into her flesh like Braille by the rumbling of his chest so close behind her—was full of speculation and promise. And her mind was suddenly filled with thoughts she shouldn't be having.

Of a late-night visit to the chalet on the end.

Of whether he'd open the door before she knocked.

Of whether his bed could fit two.

Not a question she'd ever imagined herself asking about the Morgan chalets. But instinct was a demanding mistress, and right now it was demanding she did not expose herself to any more risk than flying two hundred and fifty metres above a shark-infested ocean.

What did she want, exactly?

'I don't want to waste any more of your time if our answer is going to be no.'

And suddenly the prospect of him actually leaving ballooned large in her consciousness. These might be the last hours she'd have with him. Her fingers curled more tightly around the harness. As though it was his hand.

'I told you,' he murmured. 'It hasn't been a waste.'

Slowly, subtly, she felt the tug on the harness change direction.

'Are you ready for it to be over?'

She gasped. Could he read her mind?

'Danny's taking us back,' he breathed down on her.

Oh. No, she wasn't ready—but what possible excuse could she give him for staying up here for ever? Other than wanting it so? 'He probably wants his turn.'

'You've got him pegged already.'

The tug of descent against their straps was subtle but undeniable. Time to go back to the real world.

'What do you do up here when you're on your own?'

'Think...' His heart hammered against her back. 'Breathe, mostly. The rest of the world is a long way away from here.'

Elliott concentrated on the descent, freeing Laney to concentrate on him, and on the feel of his strong thighs below hers as she practically sat in his lap thanks to the orientation of the harnesses. He smelled salty, the sun's heat simmered in his thick wetsuit as she leaned back into him, and his mumured instructions to Danny—who couldn't possibly hear them—rumbled in his chest.

Misfit's engine got louder and louder and then Elliott tensed and bent to her ear. 'Ready, Laney? Straighten your legs and don't go to the ground. Just start running when you feel the sand. Stay upright.'

She pushed her pelvis forward to force her legs into a downward position and immediately missed the comfort and security of Elliott's body curled around hers. But landing safely pushed those thoughts from her head and she set her legs moving the moment she felt his begin to run.

And then there was sand.

And then there was *a lot* of sand.

Her legs, deprived for so long of natural blood flow, and taken by surprise by its sudden return, instantly turned to a blaze of pins and needles and gave way completely the moment they were faced with actual gravity.

Her tumble meant she snarled Elliott's legs and he tumbled, too, and the two of them were tugged along the sand for some distance by the still buoyant sail.

Finally it dumped them in a tangle of limbs, harnesses and cords before settling to the sandbar.

'*Oof*—' Elliott's sudden weight across her pushed the air from her lungs and ejected the mouthful of sand she'd ended up with.

'Are you okay?'

Close and breathy. And urgent. And very masculine, pressing down on top of her.

She struggled against the singing of her skin. And

the creativity of her imagination. 'Are you asking about my dignity?'

The chuckle rumbled from his body into hers. 'I'm asking about your bones and internal organs.'

She surveyed them all briefly as he untangled more of the harness. Everything seemed to move as it should. 'All intact, I think. Unlike my pride.'

He paused. 'Well, don't worry. This isn't my finest moment either.'

'At least I'm not witness to your humiliation.'

'No, but bloody Danny is. I won't hear the end of it.'

Sure enough, unbridled laughter drifted towards them on the lap of waves coming from the boat. He levered his weight off her and pushed to his feet, then reached down and took her hand. She was upright in a moment.

'Send me up with him, then, and let's see how *he* does, landing with a potato sack strapped to his chest.'

'No chance.'

The vehemence in his voice took her by surprise. Standing this close to him, it wasn't hard to orientate her face up to his.

'Was I actually dangerous?' Had she put Elliott at risk?

'No. I wouldn't leave you alone with him for fifteen seconds, let alone fifteen minutes.'

'Why not? Isn't he your friend?'

Methodical hands brushed the sand off the rest of her—methodical, yet somehow not…indifferent. And still super-warm.

'Yes, and I know him too well to trust him with you. I could barely trust myself. Why are you smiling?'

Because she liked knowing that their flight had been challenging for him too. 'I doubt it would have been the same with Danny. He's smaller than you. It would have been a totally different fit.'

A hint of a choke coloured his voice. 'You could tell that from shaking his hand?'

'He went out of his way to press against me when he helped me onto the boat. I just extrapolated outwards. Am I wrong?'

'No,' he breathed. 'You never are.'

They stood there, still partly bound together though the parachute no longer tethered them in a tangled mess. The masculine scent of him swilled around her despite the gentle ocean breeze, stealing the air from her lungs. And all she could think about was kissing him.

This was exactly the right moment for it, and he'd virtually warned her that it would be coming.

Her lips parted.

'So, was it everything you hoped for?'

'Wh…What?' Disappointment surged through her at conversation instead of kissing.

'The flight.'

'Oh. Yes, definitely. You're very lucky you get to do this regularly.'

He plucked a strand of windblown hair from her face and the echo of his touch tingled against her skin. Okay, so he was working his way up to a kiss.

'Not too regularly. I don't want it to ever stop feeling special.'

She licked her salt-coated lips and teased him. 'Oh, that's right. *The build-up is the best bit.*'

'You don't believe me?'

'On the contrary.' Right now she found it totally believable.

He shuffled in the sand. 'Put your arms out, Laney.'

Deep and low. And typically demanding. But she complied because she wanted nothing more this very moment than to wrap her arms around all his heat. She gave them an extra hint of width to accommodate his big body. And then she held her breath.

Nothing happened, and then…canvas and buckles clanked in a big pile into her outstretched arms.

'Hang on to this and I'll guide you back to the boat.'

Disappointment surged in where tingles had been only moments before as she curled her arms around the tangle of harness to stop it from falling straight through onto the sandbar.

Seriously? No snatched moment like in the car earlier? No taking advantage of post-flight euphoria? Just…back on the boat? But she wasn't about to beg, and she sure wasn't going to let him see her disappointment. She averted her eyes and concentrated on taking as good care of the harness as the harness had taken of her.

But instead of holding out his forearm for her to take, Elliott curled his fingers through hers in a good old-fashioned hand-hold and led her towards the splash of the surf.

'The water's clear,' he murmured. 'And the boat is a ten-metre wade out. When we get there I'll pull you up.'

They passed Danny midway, coming in for his turn, and Laney threw him a big smile of gratitude for piloting the boat for her amazing experience. She hoped he was too absorbed in himself to examine the smile too closely, in case it looked as hollow as it felt.

She shouldn't care.

She certainly shouldn't let one absent kiss suck all the joy from her otherwise amazing afternoon. She'd taken her first speedboat trip. She'd *flown*, for crying out loud—hovered two hundred and fifty metres above the world like one of her bees on the breeze. That already made this day exceptional.

A kiss would have been wasted on it, really.

Elliott let go of her hand and placed it on *Misfit*'s hull and Laney felt the dip and slap of the boat as he hauled himself up into it. A moment later he relieved her of her harness and a moment after that he was back, both hands strong and sure in hers as he pulled her up to safety, her feet walking up the hull of the boat and then over the edge. She slid down the length of his body until cool deck pressed into her feet.

Totally wasted...

Yep. She'd just keep telling herself that.

CHAPTER NINE

AMAZING HOW EXHAUSTED she felt, given she'd pretty much done nothing but sit—or hang in space—all day. Must be the sea air. Elliott had taken his time giving his friend a good run on the parasail and she'd snuggled down in the boat's comfortable leather seats and enjoyed the sea air.

As she'd slid down the length of Elliott reboarding *Misfit* she'd realised his wetsuit hung, unzipped, from his hips—which had given her a startling but not entirely unwelcome flesh memory of broad shoulders, firm chest and belly, and the strong arms that had hauled her up out of the water onto the boat. And that was how she 'saw' him now. As a sensory memory of heat and salt and smell and soft skin over firm muscle.

Who needed vision?

'You still awake?'

She turned towards the honey tones of his voice in his comfortable Audi. 'Yes.'

'Your eyes were closed.'

Her smile was as lazy as his voice. 'Takes energy, keeping them open.'

'Have I worn you out?'

'Just about. It's a good feeling.'

'Why do you have your eyelids open at all?' he asked. 'Generally speaking.'

'The natural resting place for eyelids is half closed, and that seems to creep sighted people out, so when I was little Mum just trained me to open them up, regardless.'

'For the comfort of others?'

For her survival. 'My entire childhood was a push-pull between my mother wanting to help me fit in and my father ensuring I never could.'

Whoops… Had she said that out loud? Clearly she was more tired than she'd realised. Certainly she hadn't meant it to sound so bitter.

'My mother was the very definition of "don't rock the boat",' he said. 'That's not exactly what you want in a parent either. A little fight is a good thing.'

'A little, maybe.'

'You came out okay.'

'Chalk it up to my mother's moderating influence.'

'Something else to be grateful to her for, then. I get to look into your eyes when we speak.'

'Even though I'm not in there?'

His pause went on for moments. 'Laney, just because you can't see me doesn't mean I can't see you.' He cleared his throat. 'At least I try to.'

'Really?'

'Do you imagine your eyes don't carry intelligence? Meaning? Or that they're not a window to who you are?'

'Honestly, I don't know what to imagine. I have no idea what someone would see in someone else's eyes, sighted or otherwise. Aren't they just…eyes?'

'Oh, no. Not at all.'

'What do eyes do that's so interesting?'

'They sparkle. They challenge. They contradict. They lie. They reveal. They pretty much show what someone is feeling regardless of what they are saying.'

That sounded awful. 'How do you keep a secret?'

'Some people don't.'

'So the whole "window to your soul" thing is actually true? I thought it was just a pithy saying.'

'Depends on whether there's much of a soul to be seen.'

Flat. Almost lifeless. Was he thinking about someone in particular?

'It's different, though, right? Knowing I can't see you back?'

'It's different, yes. But not worse necessarily.'

She turned fully towards him, as if the change of angle would help her pick up more of the vibes he unintentionally gave off. 'You think it's better that I can't see you?'

'If you're asking me whether I'd prefer to be able to make actual eye contact with you, yeah, of course I would. I'd love to be able to look in your eyes and have you *see* me. Read me. Know me. But too much eye contact is confrontational for most people. Sometimes you want to really look at a person but you can't because it's socially inappropriate.'

'And you can look all you want at me?'

'Your eyes are busy doing a lot of interesting other stuff when they're not seeing,' he murmured. 'And they tell me a lot more about you than you necessarily do.'

She turned her face back to the oncoming road, screening him from the very organs that they'd been discussing. She wasn't sure how she felt about him being able to *see* her quite that much. It felt like an unfair advantage.

'Why would my body use my eyes without my consent?'

'Why does a blind woman use any of the facial expressions you use? Expressions you've never seen or learned. Clearly some things are just innate. Joy and anger and unhappiness—'

She frowned again.

'—and consternation. Yep, you use that one a lot. I think the rest of us grow up learning how to disguise our expressions more than anything, so yours—when you have them—flash in neon.'

'Neon?'

'Bright light.'

'Not literally, I assume?'

His chuckle warmed her through.

'No, not literally. But they're very...honest. Do you want a real world example?'

Yes. Yes, she did.

'Today, on the sandbar, you were disappointed I didn't kiss you.'

She shot upright in her seat and only then realised how comfortable she'd become in it. 'I was not!'

'Yeah, you were. I could tell.'

'No, you couldn't.'

'You worked hard to school your features, but your eyes screamed disappointment.'

Oh, and didn't he sound pleased with himself about that?

'They did not...' But it wasn't very convincing, even to her own ears.

'I wanted to kiss you,' he murmured.

Air was sucked into her lungs. 'Why didn't you?'

'Because of something Danny said. It made it feel not right.'

Danny, who hadn't had a single meaningful thing to say all day? 'Danny told you not to kiss me?'

'Danny told me not to take advantage of you. In the afterglow of the flight. And it got me thinking. When I kiss you again I want you to be one hundred per cent present and clear-headed. Not all dosed up with adrenaline.'

When. Not *if.*

She folded her arms across her chest. 'You're assuming a lot. I'm not sure I want to kiss you again.'

'Yeah, you do.' His voice was rich with a smile.

Yeah. She did. She dropped her head and cursed under her breath. 'How do any of you have any privacy?'

'We spend a lot of time not looking at each other, I guess—'

No doubt.

'And not being entirely honest with each other.'

'Clearly a survival strategy I need to work on.' Though how exactly did one begin to train eyes that had gone rogue not to give away her deepest secrets? And who knew she'd still find anything in life yet to be perfected?

'Don't joke, Laney. Your honesty is a strength, not a weakness.'

'It's a vulnerability.'

'You don't want to be vulnerable?'

'I don't care for being exposed.'

The concept hung out there, thick and real.

'Fair enough. How about this? Whenever I'm reading your face I'll let you know. So we'll be equal.'

'So I'll at least know if my privacy is being breached?'

'Come on, Laney. It's not like you don't read the slight tone-shifts in my voice or the temperature-changes in my skin.'

She laughed at the thought.

'I give you my word, as a gentleman, that I will be honest with you about what I'm thinking and seeing when I look at you. If you'll extend me the same courtesy about reading me.'

'I'm always honest with you.'

'You don't lie. That's not necessarily the same thing.'

His words sank in. He had a point. She *did* read people—read Elliott—in a dozen ways he probably wasn't aware of, so was it really any different from him reading whatever messages her eyes were apparently giving off?

Honesty wasn't really all that much to ask for. Or to expect.

She took a deep breath. 'Okay. Can we start right now?'

'Sure.' Though he'd never sounded less sure.

'I feel like you're working up to kissing me now, and I...'

Ugh, honesty wasn't much fun.

'And you don't want that?'

'No.'

Hurt tinged his words like a barely perceptible harmonic. 'Can I ask why?'

She took a deep breath. 'Because I've decided to take matters into my own hands. Kiss you. Tonight, at the chalet. And I've kind of talked myself into how that's going to go.'

The hurt morphed into a tightness. 'And how *is* it going to go?'

She lifted her chin. 'Really well.'

Maybe eyes did a lot more than he'd said, because she was pretty sure she could feel his boring heat into her very soul.

'Far be it from me to ruin a good plan.'

Laney checked in with her parents so they knew she was back and then begged off to go and have a much needed shower. To wash the salt from her skin and hair. To make herself beautiful. Not that she knew what that was or, until today, why anyone would bother.

But now she got it.

This was why they bothered. This gorgeous anticipation.

She wanted Elliott to open that chalet door and see her standing there looking pretty. Better than pretty, really. But short of inviting her mother in here and explaining what she was up to that wasn't going to happen. And if she trusted Owen with the task she couldn't guarantee what she'd end up looking like. So she'd just have to work with what she had. Kelly had used her as test dummy enough times that she left a small make-up kit in her bedroom perpetually, the contents personalised to her, and she hunted it down now and quickly fingered her way through it, opening lids and testing the contents. Isolating the bits she recognised.

Mascara. Lip-gloss. Loose powder. All past their best-by date, probably.

Not much she could do wrong with any of them if she was careful. Even so, it took her an eternity to apply them, and she was conscious the whole time of Elliott sitting in his chalet, wondering if she'd forgotten. Or just chickened out.

She almost did. Twice. But determination had

never been her weak point, so she ran her brush through her hair one last time and whistled for Wilbur. He came running in from the other room, all toasty and sleepy from the fire, a disbelieving little yowl in his voice when she produced his harness.

'We won't be outside for long,' she promised. 'Then you'll be warm again.'

And so would she. Extremely warm. Fingers crossed.

The audacity of what she was about to do hit her then. A clandestine meeting with a man. A man from the city. A man she might not see again after this weekend.

But then wasn't that part of the attraction? And the excitement? And she was twenty-five years old. It was time.

'Hey…' She poked her head around Owen's bedroom door.

The rustling told her he was pushing to his feet. 'What do you need?'

'Nothing. Just…is my face okay?'

Ugh… How ridiculous.

Confusion coloured his response. 'Compared to who?'

'No. I mean, does it look okay? Nothing out of place?'

'Is that—?'

'Forget it.'

'No…wait. Are you wearing *make-up*?'

'Is it or isn't it applied correctly?'

'Is.' Typical Owen shorthand. 'Did you do it yourself?'

'Yes.' Why else would she be humiliating herself like this?

'Why?'

'Thanks, O.'

'Wait—!'

But no way was she going to explain a thing to her twin brother.

Wilbur hurried her more than usual through the still garden and she barely had to tell him where they were going. As if it was such a given. Within minutes her knuckles were on the glossy wood of Elliott's door.

'Hey,' he breathed as warm air spilled out onto her. 'I thought maybe you'd changed your mind.'

'Sorry, I was—' *obsessing like a teenager over something that probably doesn't matter* '—caught up.'

'Your parents?'

'No, they've gone to bed.'

'Come on in. It's cold.'

Wilbur didn't wait to be asked twice and Elliott

chuckled as he scrambled in, claws clattering on the timber floors.

'Watch yourself,' Elliott muttered as he helped her up the steps. 'There are candles…well, pretty much everywhere.'

'Where did you get candles?' Though what she really wanted to ask was why.

'I found a packet of tealights in the bottom drawer. For power outages, presumably.'

'And you thought I'd enjoy them?' she teased.

'I thought I'd enjoy looking at you in candlelight.'

'Well, that seems to be a waste of perfectly good make-up, then.'

He stopped so suddenly she walked right into him. 'You put make-up on?'

'You can't tell?'

His heat increased marginally as he stepped closer. 'Is that strawberry lip-gloss?'

Really? He had to ask? The scent of it was pulsing off her.

'Some kind of berry.' Her tongue dashed across her lips without being asked. 'It's very sweet.'

Elliott's voice dropped to a half-growl. 'I'll bet.'

In the silence Wilbur harrumphed and found himself a comfortable spot to flop down.

'So, where are all these candles?'

'Just avoid anything above elbow-height; that should do it.'

'That's not all that helpful.'

His low chuckle tickled the hairs on her whole body. 'Okay, how about we just sit on the sofa.'

Sofas were generally candle-free. 'Okay.'

'Anything you need I'll bring to you. This is a full service date.'

'Is it a date?'

'I consider this a continuation of the first date, so…yeah.'

'Okay.'

Wow. She was rocking the vocab tonight.

'Wine?'

Her, 'Yes, please!' was almost unseemly in its haste. But when Elliott pressed a glass stem into her hand and she lifted it to her lips she discovered the rather dramatic downside to flavoured lip-gloss. 'Ugh, this wine is *not* enhanced by berry flavour.'

'Hang on,' he said. 'I'll get you something to take it off with.'

She felt the coffee table to her left and placed her glass down as he pushed out of his seat. But then his hands were at her shoulders, gently pressing her back into the sofa, and his lips were close against hers.

'I seem to be out of make-up wipes,' he murmured.

Did such a thing even exist? Her voice was mostly a chuckle. 'Shame...'

Hot lips pressed down onto hers, sliding against the gloss and roaming over her mouth. She arched up out of the sofa to meet them more fully. Hazy heat swelled up and dazzled her senses as Elliott kissed her, mouthing her the way she'd wanted so desperately on the sandbar—tasting and exploring and teasing—torturing her tongue with his. His arms slid around behind her and kept her hard up against him.

It was like the parasailing again, but her position was reversed. She sighed into his mouth.

But then he relaxed her into the sofa-back and lifted his head. 'There—that's sorted it.'

For a moment she was too disorientated to speak, but she forced her wits back into line as she straightened in her seat. Back upright like a regular person. 'Are you now wearing it?'

His laugh was mostly snort. 'My sleeve is'

'You're worse than Owen.' Her wine returned magically into her hand. 'So that's the kissing over with, then?'

Boo.

'It really wasn't my plan to maul you the moment

you walked in the door...' He sounded genuinely confused.

'But you couldn't resist?'

'Opportunity presented itself.' He leaned into the sofa more fully but his voice didn't leave her for a moment. He stayed close. 'And what kind of a host would I be to leave you without assistance? But I haven't forgotten what you said, so I give you my word the next kiss is entirely up to you.'

If it was up to her then she'd like to resume kissing right now, actually. But social niceties made that impossible.

Her breath shuddered in quietly. 'So I just wanted to say thank you, again, for today. Parasailing was amazing.'

'I agree. It's going to be hard to go back to solo lifts.'

'You're so lucky you get to do that whenever you want.'

'Whenever work lets me.'

'You work weekends?'

'I'm working *this* weekend.'

Work. That was like a bucket of cold lip-gloss. 'Oh.'

'Tomorrow, I mean. Not today—definitely not now. But, yes, that's the sad truth about the lifestyle. You spend so much time funding it you can't always be free to enjoy it.'

'Guess that's the difference between your job and mine. I live my love every day.'

'If I wanted to do that I'd have to become a para-sailing instructor.'

'Would that be so bad? You're very good at it.'

He gave that his usual thought. 'I'm pretty sure Ashmore Coolidge wouldn't let me go without a fight. And I'd have to move out of my penthouse. And I don't know how long I could go before I would feel like I was under-achieving. You know?'

Back to the *realising*. 'Isn't doing what you love fulfilling your potential?'

'Not if it's not making you decent money.'

'What about being happy?'

'I'll be happy when I'm retired.'

'No, you won't. You'll be appalled at how much time you have and how much money you might otherwise be making with that time.'

His chuckle warmed her even more than his closeness. 'Yeah, probably.'

Conversation dropped off and Laney fought her natural inclination to flinch when soft fingers lifted a lock of her hair and draped it back, away from her face.

'I can see the make-up now,' he murmured.

Yeah, she'd bet he could. He was leaning close enough. 'Did I do it right?'

'I can barely tell it's there. Which is probably the point.' The sofa-back shifted as he did. 'You always look good. Natural.'

'Thank you.'

'So tell me about this kiss you're imagining. Do you have make-up on in it?'

'When I imagine it, it's all about sensation. Not really how good we look while doing it.'

His smile warmed the conversation. 'Describe the sensations.'

Discomfort washed through her. 'Um…'

He helped. 'Is it fast or slow?'

Yeah, this would be easier. 'Slow.'

'Why?'

'So it will last.'

His small grunt said *good reason*.

'What else?'

'You're standing. So I have to stretch up to you.' And press her body against his—but she wasn't going to share that part.

'Sounds like a lot of work on your part.'

'I don't mind. It's worth it.'

He liberated the wine glass from her and it clanked on the coffee table. Then strong arms pulled her to her feet and he stepped in close. She had to tilt her head to avoid her nose pressing into his chest.

'A good kiss, then?' he murmured.

'Yep. Just right.'

Gentle hands lifted hers up and linked them behind his neck. Her body pressed against his, just as it had in her mind. Warm and soft met hot and hard. His hands slid around onto her hips.

'And what's *just right* to you, Goldilocks?' Ragged breath totally betrayed his interest, no matter how casual the hold of his arms.

Speech was almost impossible past the tight press of her chest. 'Lazy. Explorative.'

'Who controls it?' This breathed right against her lips.

'Me, at first.' She took a long, slow breath. 'But then you.'

He immediately suspended his descent. Froze there. Waiting. 'Then it's your move, Laney.'

Yeah.

Only real kisses weren't quite as easy as fantasy ones. Every breath pulled in her chest, like Wilbur against his harness when he wanted to be released. But Elliott's patient silence and oh-so-warm body encouraged her, and she feathered her fingertips up his jaw to rest on his cheek, then pushed up onto her toes to make contact. It didn't matter that they'd already kissed—that had been *him* kissing her.

This was *her*...

Initiating a kiss for the first time.

Her lips fluttered as they met his—half missing his mouth, but all the more exciting for landing so squarely on his full bottom lip by mistake. She loved that bottom lip, though her experience of it was somewhat limited. She hoped to get to know it a whole lot more. A hint of stubble below it scraped her own hyper-sensitive flesh and Elliott's arms tightened around her, slid up to entwine them and trap her within his embrace.

The security of his hold gave her courage a boost, and she pressed her kiss more firmly against his receptive mouth, lapping gently at his closed lips until they gave her the access she wanted.

Elliott bound her closer—into a space she hadn't even realised could exist—and tangled her tongue with his, challenging her to yield. Fighting for control was fun, but ceding to his experience was a pleasure, and she whimpered as he took over the exploration, roaming and tasting and tormenting with his talented mouth.

It was just as she'd imagined. Yet so much more.

'And then what happens?' he ground out as he rose for breath.

She tipped her spinning head.

'In your perfect kiss, Laney? What comes next?'

'I don't know. I haven't let myself think beyond that.'

She felt his immediate tension everywhere. It pressed against her. The subtle tightening of his muscles even as they loosened—just as subtly—their hold on her.

'You haven't let yourself or you don't know what comes next?' His hold loosened even further at her silence. 'Have you ever slept with anyone, Laney?'

Her mind spiralled in a slow circle, making thinking difficult. 'Wilbur.'

'Not counting your dog.' He chuckled.

Then, no. 'Why? Does that make a difference?'

He released her that little bit further. 'Yeah, it does. Of course it does.'

'I'm twenty-five, Elliott. It has to happen eventually.'

She really wanted it to happen eventually. Actually, she kind of wanted it to happen now. While her body was still on board with that plan.

Those lips that had just tortured hers so perfectly shaped new words. Final words.

'But not tonight.'

* * *

She placed one foot behind her to steady herself as her stretch shrank backwards. Away from Elliott.

Here it comes...

Confusion stained her pretty face. 'You're not attracted to me?'

'Laney...'

'That's a genuine question, Elliott.'

Yeah. She wasn't the fishing for compliments type. 'It's not about attraction, Laney. It's about appropriateness.'

Half the extra colour birthed by their kisses drained from her face. 'What?'

His stomach fisted hard, deep in his body. 'Sleeping with you would be...'

'Inappropriate?'

Just do it, man. It was always going to end like this. Of course it was.

'Unethical.'

That word—that sentiment—had her taking a second step back. The coffee table hit her calves. But she stabilised and straightened. 'Isn't that something you should have thought about before all the kissing started?'

'Look, Laney. There's a big difference between kissing someone and taking their virginity.'

One meant something. The other meant *every-thing*. And he didn't do *everything*.

Her arms crept around her torso. 'So if I wasn't a virgin we'd be having sex right now?'

Would they? Would his galloping confusion be any less if he was not her first? Or would his conscience still have raised its unwelcome head.

He sighed and turned partly away. 'No. There's still a difference.'

And his brain had been trying to get his attention as he'd paced up and down in the little chalet, waiting for her to arrive, but his body had kept overruling it. Because he wanted to be able to want her. So badly.

'Who's going to know?'

'I'll know, Laney. That's not the kind of man I am.'

'Really? The kind of man that would lead a woman on and then drop her cold?'

He couldn't say he didn't deserve that. Except he discovered he couldn't say anything at all.

'Why not have someone else assigned to Morgan's?' she suggested finally. 'Nothing inappropriate then.'

And he'd have jumped on that if it were the only thing stopping him. If it weren't for the raging tightness deep in his chest. But she was handing him the perfect out and he was coward enough to take it.

'Because you're my case.'

'Sure—normally. But under the circumstances...'

'No one else wants you, Laney. I'm the one pushing Morgan's at executive level.'

Speaking of pushing...something was driving him hard. Pushing Laney back. Pushing her away as determinedly as he'd dragged her towards him only minutes before.

'But if they agree we have potential? Wouldn't someone else run with that?'

Everything he'd worked for over so many years suddenly felt unstable—unreliable and totally out of his control—and that big, gaping void inside him seemed to loom large and hollow.

'I don't want someone else running with it. Morgan's is my client. *My* opportunity.'

She sagged down onto the coffee table and the rest of her colour abandoned her. 'Opportunity for what?'

Surely she'd understand... This was Laney. She was amazing. If anyone could understand him, what drove him—

'I've been gunning for partner for two years, Laney. And Morgan's is going to get me there. I'm not about to pass that opportunity off to someone else, even for—'

He caught himself, but the sentiment hung out there, all miserable and unmissable. *Even for a blind woman.*

Her fingers curled on the table-edge just as they had on his boat.

'For me?'

Hurting her hurt him. It was like an open wound in his body. But something stopped him from going to her. Some ancient fear. Some inherent…*lack.* When all he wanted to do was trust someone with the truth.

Trust Laney with the big void inside him.

'I see. So the kissing? The parasailing?'

'I wanted to get to know you, Laney. I still do. I really wasn't thinking about what would happen next.'

'You've filled the place with *candles.* And you had a couple of hours to think about it…'

He opened his mouth to defend the undefendable. So he just closed it again.

Her spine forced her upright, rigid and erect. 'Your career means more to you than an opportunity to take things further with me?'

No. That wasn't it at all. But lying was easier than trying to untangle the truth when the truth was so deeply woven into his flesh. 'My career *is* important to me,' he hedged.

She pressed her palms to her cheeks, as if that could mask the dread now there.

'Laney, don't look like that.'

'There is no way this could have worked,' she whispered. 'We're such different people...'

'No, we're not. But the timing is all off.'

Her head came up. 'How is time going to change anything?'

'Circumstances could change.'

Misery thickened her voice and deadened her eyes. 'I told you Morgan's isn't interested.'

'You haven't heard my proposal yet.'

'I don't really need to, Elliott. We're just not interested.'

'Wait until you see the numbers.'

'Like that's all that matters.' But then her face lifted. 'If Morgan's was not an Ashmore Coolidge client any more...could we keep seeing each other?'

'You'd *fire* us?'

'I can get anyone to do our financial management.'

The implication being she couldn't find just anyone to make her feel the way he did. His heart hammered dangerously faster.

'Just so we could be together?'

* * *

And there it was.

The great imbalance in their respective feelings and attitudes made manifest in that one little word.

Just.

Laney would have done almost anything to give them a chance to explore this thing between them more. Elliott would do virtually nothing.

She shot back to her feet. Angry enough to stir. 'So, a one-night stand, then?'

Not that she had any intention of doing anything of the sort.

Anger hissed out of him. 'I told you. It's—'

'Unethical. I know. But that's a relationship. I'm talking about a one-off thing. No strings attached.' She waved her hands wildly around her. 'What happens in the chalet stays in the chalet.'

'Laney—'

'Come on, Elliott. Throw a girl a bone. I want to get it out of the way.'

'Laney… You're angry.'

Fury boiled from down deep inside. 'Yeah, I'm angry! You started the whole touchy-feely thing. You with your interesting conversation and gorgeous smell and gentle touch. Why even start it if you knew you couldn't do anything with what happened?'

'Because I didn't think anything *would* happen. I thought it was safe.'

Her snort startled a collar-jangle out of Wilbur. 'To mess with a blind girl?'

'To get to know you. To have you get to know me. To enjoy it.'

Natural justice ran strong in her. She couldn't really stand here and criticise him for not thinking it though when she'd totally failed to do so. She was just so caught up in him.

'Why bother?' Except it hit her then. Exactly why he'd bothered. 'Or did you think it would improve your chances of us saying yes if we'd all come to like you?'

She couldn't bring herself to say *I*. She could barely manage 'like'. Because somewhere this weekend she'd gone flying past 'like' as surely as if she was back in that parasailing harness.

What she felt for Elliott Garvey had stopped being 'like' a half-dozen conversations ago.

Not that it mattered now. Except to name exactly what it was she could never show him.

'At first, maybe. It's good business to build a good working relationship with clients.'

'Do you have dinner with all your clients? Drink wine and share stories?'

'Yeah. Pretty much.'

'Do you kiss them all too? Take them up into the sky and press your body against them?'

Who knew? Maybe he did...

'That's not why I took you parasailing.'

'Then why did you? You called it a date.'

He sighed. 'That's what it felt like.'

'So why do it?'

'Because you wanted to. And because I—'

'Because you what?'

'Because I wanted you to get off this farm. I wanted you to try something new and see that it wasn't so earth-shattering.'

Something cold sliced in under her diaphragm. And the hole it left sucked every bit of joy out of the day they'd just shared. Breakfast, the research lab, the flight, the kissing.

Yet earth-shattering was exactly what it had been.

'You thought one train trip to the city and an afternoon boating was going to make me change my mind about taking Morgan's global? How much of a hick do you think I am?'

'Be honest, Laney. Your horizons are bounded by ocean, trees and a small town. It doesn't hurt to stretch them a little.'

Offence blazed large and real in her chest. 'I was just spending time with you. I didn't realise I was signing up for a self-improvement class.'

Though now she could clearly see what today had really all been about. And what that meant Elliott thought of her.

Nice girl. Smart and business savvy. Good kisser. *Charmingly provincial.*

'You think that taking me to the big smoke and spoiling me with experiences, getting me to trust you, was going to change my mind? I'm not that shallow, Elliott.'

Though it looked as if maybe he was. Disappointment leaked in with all the hurt.

'No, you're not. But you are—above all else—unfailingly sensible and loyal to Morgan's. I was counting on you wanting the best for them. Regardless of your own fears.'

She reeled back as if he truly had slapped her clean across the face. 'Is that what you think? That I'm afraid?'

He took both her hands in his, gave them a little shake. 'You shouldn't be. You are amazing. You can do anything.'

Snatching them back caused a suck of breath from him. Seriously—he was *still* campaigning? 'Just because I can doesn't mean I should!'

She turned and fumbled with her hands for the nearest grabbable surface, but only encountered a tealight full of molten wax. It spilled as she upended the tiny candle in her haste and she stumbled away from the pain. But of course it only went with her.

Life in a nutshell, really.

'Laney, let me—'

'No!'

Her bark drew Wilbur to her side and he leaned against her leg, where she could more easily reach the handle on his harness. She grabbed it like the lifeline it was. Hardening wax and all.

'I thought you understood me.' *I thought you liked me.* 'But you're just like all the others. Humouring me.'

Using me.

She thought back on how she'd been with him. How vulnerable she'd let herself be.

'This was a mistake.' Emotion thrummed through her voice. 'Something between you and me could never have worked.'

No matter how good the kisses were. Or how he made her laugh. Or how attracted she was to his brain. *Damn it.*

'Laney, let me walk you back to the house.'

'I'm fine. I have Wilbur.' There was one male in her life, at least, who accepted her for who she was and was always there for her. Unfailingly.

'Will I see you tomorrow?' he risked.

She threw her arm out and found the doorframe

before feeling her way down to the handle. 'Where else am I going to go with such diminished horizons?'

'Come on, Laney—'

She swung the door open, tiredly, and stepped down off the step. 'Leave it, Elliott. Let's just get back to the real reason for your presence.' For every single thing he'd done here. 'Back to business.'

'I don't want to leave it like this.'

'Well, too bad. It's not your call. I'm a bit over doing what other people want of me. Now I'm doing what I want. And what I want is to end this conversation and get the hell out of your cabin.'

And his life.

She nudged Wilbur on with more force than he deserved and he shot forward in apology. Guilt immediately washed through her.

'Sorry, pup,' she whispered as he led her back through the silent paddock towards the house. Towards privacy. Towards her long, lonely future.

As if being physically blind weren't difficult enough… Now she could add social blindness to her list of challenges.

How could she not have realised which way the wind was blowing? Elliott had made it perfectly clear how important his work was to him and how fully he was backing his proposal. But she'd looked right past the obvious the moment a man came along who appeared to understand her.

Pretended to, perhaps?

Yet for all his corporate gloss, charming words and plain yummy smell, Elliott Garvey was just like all those other men she'd dated. In it for number one. And feeling disappointed and disillusioned was painful enough without also feeling like the blindest blind woman ever to have stumbled on the earth.

Although there was one benefit to having no vision—it made no difference to how fast you could move while tears streamed down your face.

CHAPTER TEN

WHAT A MORON. He really couldn't have messed things up any better.

Any worse.

Elliott moved quietly behind Laney as she showed him the final remaining area of Morgan's operations. Her movements were as dull as her expression. As carefully distant. Closed to any further discussion outside of the necessary.

Utterly closed to him.

And why wouldn't she be? Everything she'd said last night was right. He shouldn't have started anything with her without knowing where and how it was going to end. He didn't do unevaluated risk. He did strategic risk. Carefully measured risk.

He absolutely didn't do head-swimming, mind-addling, resolve-defying risk.

Because this was how it ended.

Enjoying Laney's company was an indulgence, and kissing her had turned out to be a luxury he couldn't afford. But it was because of his personal values—not his corporate ones. Ashmore Coolidge was an old-school boys' club. They wouldn't have given a toss about one of their team sleeping with a client if it meant closing the deal. Actually, in truth, they would have had *a lot* to say behind closed doors—especially with a client as young and attractive *and blind* as Laney—but none of it would have been negative. Unless it had lost the deal, of course.

And he wasn't about to lose the deal. He was a realiser. Not a loser. Without his professional success, what did he have?

Just him, his nice apartment, and the big vacant place inside him.

Laney finally wrestled free the front base cover on one of the hives in the stack they were looking at. Her fingers dusted over the front of it.

'When the slide is in this position—' she lowered it '—access to the hive is uninterrupted. But when I raise it—' she did so '—the bees have to go through the collection plate to get inside.'

'It's tight,' he said, really just so that he could gauge her reaction to him. So that she had to engage with him and not just deliver some kind of professional monologue.

'That's how we harvest the pollen. They have to drop the biggest bundles in order to get through with the rest. Then we sell it to the commercial food industry.'

Her eyes were utterly lifeless. And that was when he realised just how full of life they usually were—if you took the time to look for it.

'They don't sound too happy.'

'They don't like change.'

'Or having to work doubly hard to bring in their quota?'

She turned. Finding criticism where he'd intended none, judging by her unhappy expression.

'I would have thought that was right up your alley? Maximising their output. No wasted potential.'

Yeah, it was. But it wasn't like *her*. So there had to be a good reason. 'Is pollen lucrative?'

Her frustrated sigh was telling. 'Yeah. It is.'

Like everything bee-related except maybe honey.

'But that's not why you do it?'

'I do it because we can freeze it and feed it back to the hive during winter to sustain them. It means fewer deaths in winter.'

Death in winter. That was about the most perfect opening he was going to get to talk about his expansion ideas. But that freckle-kissed face was not open to ideas. Not right now.

Maybe never. Not to him.

'That makes more sense.'

Because Laney just wasn't about the money. Or the market. She was all about the bees. Bees and family. And maybe those two things were one in her mind.

'I'm glad. I would hate to be doing something you didn't understand.'

Wow. Sarcasm really didn't sit well on those lips. 'Laney—'

'So anyway,' she bustled on. 'That's it. Bees in here, pollen catches there, and we empty it twice a day for a week and then they get two months off.'

Now she sounded just like the disaffected tour guide she was trying to be. All her passion gone.

And he missed the other Laney horribly. This one made her business sound like…a business. Regular Laney made it sound like her life.

But at the end of the day it was the business that he was here to talk about. Not her. Not her great love for what she did or how fascinating the various aspects of the apiary were. His job required him to stay focussed.

On getting Morgan's signed up. On getting his promotion.

'What time are we meeting your parents?' he asked, forcing himself back on track. Just as the debacle that had been last night had.

'Lunchtime.'

Noon. That was still a couple of hours away. What the hell were they going to *not* talk about for that long?

'So what's next?'

She turned to face him. 'That's it, actually. You've seen everything. I've got to get on with doing my job, so you'll have to entertain yourself until our meeting.'

Right. 'You need any help?'

'I'd say yes if I thought you could do much.'

The barb glanced off his corporate-thickened hide, but the fact she'd fired it off at all really bothered him. It was symptomatic of how much he'd hurt her last night. And he was not going to leave things like that.

'Laney. I'm really, really sorry about last night. You were right. I shouldn't have indulged myself in getting to know you better. It was unfair of me.'

She kept her face averted so he couldn't even read her accidental expressions. Only her silence.

'I should have known better,' he went on. 'And been stronger.'

She turned, straightened. 'What's the matter, Elliott? Trying to ingratiate yourself before the meeting?'

His head reeled back. Actually, it hadn't occurred

to him that last night might go against him in his presentation. Because that wasn't Laney. She loved Morgan's too much to let something personal get in the way of its success.

But there was no way she'd believe him if he told her that. 'I am trying to make good, Laney. But not because of the meeting. Just because I've hurt you. And I'm sorry.'

'Don't be. I appreciate knowing where you stand. And what you think of me.'

'I think highly of you.'

Her hands balled on her hips. 'You think I'm too afraid to step off this property.'

Every moment they spent on her deficiencies distracted him from his own.

'You have good reason to be—'

'I am not afraid!' she urged. 'And I don't need your patronising concern. I stay because I love it here. I love what I do and the way I do it. This is my home.'

This wasn't making things better. 'Okay, Laney...'

'And I don't need you to humour me, either, Elliott.' She stepped closer. 'I get it, you know. I may be inexperienced romantically, but I'm a big girl. I know what this is. You're interested. I can tell. But you're interested in your career more. That's just how it is.'

Before he could reply she barrelled onwards.

'I'm not angry that things didn't work out between us last night. I'm angry because it's revealed a barrier between us much more fundamental than geography. We have different values. Despite the chemistry. Despite everything. And all the good fit in the world can't change a person's values.'

Did she mean *his* values? As if hers weren't half the problem?

'So this isn't anger at you, Elliott. It's disappointment. And resentment that something so fundamental is in my way. And anger at myself for not being more alert for the possibility. I was just enjoying you so much.' She shuddered in a big breath and when she spoke again all the vulnerable momentum of her last words was gone. 'That's all this is. And there is nothing you can do or say to undo that. Is there?'

Sure there was. He could say, *Hey Laney...screw everything I've worked towards for years, and screw the big, freaking terrifying void inside me. Let's just see where this leads.* But he wouldn't. Because he couldn't just throw away everything he'd worked at his whole adult life. Not to address someone else's fear.

He'd walked away from that once before—left his only family rather than diminish his life down to his mother's level. And that sacrifice would be totally meaningless if he didn't keep chasing his dream.

Success challenged him and drove him. And it defined him. Without that, who the hell was he?

And it was the only thing that kept him from collapsing back into that big void inside.

'If things were different—'

'But they're not. Let's get real about that. I'm a bee farmer from the country. You're a corporate realiser from the city. And ne'er the twain shall meet.'

And there it was. Their almost-relationship fully nutshelled. She was right—it didn't matter how much either of them wanted things to be different; they were what they were.

'I'll see you at the meeting,' he murmured after a long silence.

'Yeah. You will.'

But after that…? Whether or not Morgan's went ahead with expansion, chances were good he wouldn't be seeing Laney again. Not if he wanted to be fair to her. Because the two of them couldn't spend time together and not feel this thing they had. And it was impossible to feel it and not want to act on it.

Like he did right now.

He just wanted to pull her into his hold and rest

his chin on her head and promise her that everything was going to be okay.

But he couldn't, because that would be lying.

Nothing about this was okay.

And so all he could do was leave her in this place
she loved so much, with the bees that were her life,
and trust that it could heal the damage he'd done
since arriving.

Laney gave it a full sixty seconds after Elliott's
steady, heavy footfalls on the turf had diminished
to make sure he was really gone. Then she sagged
back against the hives and buried her hands in her
face.

Not her finest moment.

None of this was Elliott's fault any more than it
was hers. They just didn't fit. This must happen to
people all over the world every day. Relationships
that had a lot going for them but suffered from
some fundamental flaw that just...*broke* them.

Not that what they had was a *relationship*, but it
had started to feel like one. Hadn't it?

Wilbur shoved his snout against her thigh and she
lowered one hand to his damp, cool nose.

'It's okay...' she murmured.

Though she was pretty sure that was what he was
trying to tell her.

Yeah, she was all right. None of her feelings were terminal. She wanted to be like everyone else, didn't she? Well, ordinary didn't come much more ordinary than heartbreak. Just another life experience she was coming to late in life.

Her own thought stopped her cold.

Was her heart *broken*?

She peered inwards. Yep, just like the big divot that Owen had put in their ute last year when he was jack-arsing around. Nice and dented but nothing terminal.

Except the deeper ache still bothered her. The fingers of her imagination probed and poked, looking for rifts that she couldn't find, but as they did so pain oozed out from below. As if the dent had damaged something much more delicate deep inside.

Hope. Self-belief. Faith. Haemorrhaging away quietly.

Yep; those were the things that had suffered most last night. That had taken such a knock. The pain of rejection she could learn to live with, but if she let him damage those essential parts of herself she'd never forgive herself.

Or Elliott.

She turned and felt her way along the hives until she reached the ones she knew were in the down phase of pollen collection. Where the bees didn't have a grudge to bear. She lifted the top two boxes off and let her hands rest on the open hive. Bees swarmed up and over her hands in a mix of surprise and curiosity—each of their soft feet a gentle, tiny kiss on her skin—until their collective weight became tangible. She slowly turned her palms up and the mass crawled around, chasing gravity, surrounding her with happy bee sounds and the comforting tickle of all their oscillating wings.

This was what she did. This was what she'd been born for. And who she was.

She had an idyllic life here on the Morgan property—a life she loved, where she was safe and happy, and where her proficiency as an apiarist gave her immense satisfaction. She'd be foolish to brush all that off like so many bees. Some people never had any of those things in their lives, let alone all of them.

So it wasn't going to come with a romantic happy-ever-after…? Three out of four was pretty darned good.

But consigning herself to a life without love didn't sit comfortably, and her gently waving fingers trembled to a bee-laden halt even as her chest squeezed down into a ball.

Love.

Did she love Elliott? Surely that took more time than they'd had?

So what if he was the first man she'd ever met who treated her like a regular person? He made allowances for her sight but he didn't treat her as if she was deficient.

Sure, he was the first man she'd kissed when she had initiated and really *wanted* his kiss. And more.

And, yes, he was the first man she'd ever met whom she truly *saw*. Both as a man and as a glorious, rich glow in the nothing of her visual perception.

And that was what she was going to miss most. Elliott was the only person other than her family that she'd ever had inside her head. Rarefied ground.

She tipped her fingers down towards the hive and gently shook most of the bees free, then turned them over and repeated the exercise. Some clung to her, exactly as she was clinging to a stupid wish that things could be different. But eventually they gave in and dropped off—just as eventually she'd realise the truth.

Elliott Garvey was going to be her 'once upon a time' man.

The man she'd kissed, once.

The man she'd gone parasailing with, once.

The man she'd started to fall in love with, once.

CHAPTER ELEVEN

'SO WHAT DO you think?'

The whole Morgan clan watched him intently except for Laney, who faced off to one side, looking for all the world as if she was a million miles away. Though Elliott knew by her stillness that she'd been concentrating one hundred per cent during his long spiel.

Wilbur snored over by the crackling fireplace.

'Surely customs issues would make it impossible?'

'Collectively, they're losing hundreds of millions of bees every year as northern winters worsen and lengthen. This is now a priority for their agricultural boards. Customs are prioritising supply from apiaries like yours.'

'Won't it be a problem that we haven't used pesticides?'

'Outweighed by the benefits of your geographic isolation and good disease rankings.'

The whole family fell to silence. He'd given them

a lot to think about. A whole new market that could be more lucrative than all their other operations put together. Shipping ready-to-go hives to the northern hemisphere in time for spring to replace their disturbingly depleted local species. Populations that were suffering from ever-worsening northern winters.

He took a breath and focussed on the only silent person in the room.

'Laney? Nothing to say?' Quite the opposite, he suspected. Something about her posture said she was fighting to hold her tongue.

'It's certainly a big market—' she said, still flat.

Even her mother looked around, frowning, at the death in Laney's tone. Then Ellen's perceptive regard came straight to him.

He couldn't return it.

'But I'm sure everyone's getting on the bandwagon.'

'Everyone doesn't have Morgan's spotless organic pedigree.'

'We'd be sending our bees overseas to die.'

Was she serious? 'After a full season of foraging. Just like they would here.'

'They're biologically adapted to do best here.'

'They don't have to do "best"—they just have

to do okay. Even okay is better than nothing when you have no other choice.'

'They *belong* here.'

The fervency of her assertion bothered him. It was as if she was talking about something much bigger than bees. *Okay...* 'You're just looking for reasons to say no.'

She sat up straighter. 'I don't like the presumption that our bees are just a product to be packed up and shipped into a biological warzone.'

'You're an apiarist, Laney. Your bees *are* a product, no matter how well you treat them while they're here.'

'What you're describing is a massive undertaking.'

'It's big in scale, sure, but you have the skills.'

'*I* do?'

'Morgan's does. And, yes, you definitely do.'

Her hands twisted in her lap and he realised, too late, that he'd said the wrong thing.

'So this comes down to me?'

He opened his mouth to respond and then discovered he didn't know what to say. So he just looked at Ellen.

'It's a family decision, love,' she ventured.

Laney's lips pressed tighter. 'But let's be realistic,

Mum. Are either of you going to want to run this? You guys are gearing up for retirement.'

There was a strange kind of agony in her voice. Controlled panic. Almost palpable. And her parents' silence was another nail in the coffin of his promotion at Ashmore Coolidge. If they weren't going to support this then he was dead in the water.

That vast nothing inside him seemed to swell and loom, almost in celebration. Had it just been waiting for everything to fall in a pile?

Laney turned back in his direction but her gaze overshot him. 'So it does come down to me, then? A massive change in direction, constant overseas travel, mountains of paperwork. All taking me away from what I love doing. Why would I do that?'

'I'll do it,' Owen said quietly.

'Between waves?' Laney snorted and didn't even bother directing it at her brother. 'No, this comes down to me. As it always was going to.'

'Your mother could help with the administration—' her father started.

'Seriously, Dad? She can barely keep up with the admin as it is.'

'You'd be making enough that you could hire someone,' Elliott pointed out.

'Laney, it could set us up—all of us—for life.'

'Aren't we already set up, Dad? What more do we need?'

'You'll need a place of your own,' he said. 'And Owen will. Then your children will, and his. What will you do? Continue to subdivide Morgan land until our descendants are living on quarter-acre blocks?'

'Children? I think we're getting ahead of ourselves a little.' She kept her words firmly averted from Elliott. Even putting them in a thought together hurt her physically. 'A couple of months ago we were thrilled with how the business was going. Now suddenly I'm being short-sighted?'

No one laughed at the poor joke.

'It's the same business, Laney,' Elliott urged. 'You just scale up and add an export arm.'

'My existing arms are kind of full,' she practically shouted back at him.

'I'll do it,' Owen tried again.

Elliott glanced at him where he sat across the room. His gaze was steady in his father's direction. The most serious he'd ever seen him.

'It would be massive, Owen,' Laney tossed back. 'Don't be ridiculous.'

He lifted one eyebrow, but then went back to watching his father. 'I'm not Superwoman over there, I realise,' he said, 'but even Helena would have to learn that side of things—why not me?'

'Because *you* would rather surf than work,' Laney dismissed him.

'Only because what we do here is boring and repetitive.'

'It's not boring!' she defended, turning her anger to him. 'It's streamlined through years of perfection.'

'It's mind-numbing, Laney. Same tasks, over and over. I'd love a chance to do something new. And to travel.'

'Helena, you can do anything you set your mind to,' Robert said, firmly dragging the conversation back to her again.

'I don't want to do it, Dad.'

'You'd be great at it.'

'Why is no one listening to me?' she urged. 'I'm not interested.'

'Take one trip,' Elliott offered. 'Come with me and meet some of the apiarists who are really struggling.'

'Why? So I can add their guilt trip to yours?'

'What guilt trip?'

'"*Come on, Laney, my promotion hinges on this*".' Her excellent impression of him was none too flattering. 'You've made it abundantly clear that you've hitched your star completely to Morgan's. And to me.'

'To you, how?'

'Please... Do you seriously expect me to believe that you wouldn't use my vision to get a point of difference in the market?'

Injustice bit low and hard. Was that what she thought of him? 'I would not.'

'I think you'd use anything at your disposal once you'd built up a bit of momentum.'

The silence grew thick. 'This isn't about me. It's about Morgan's.'

Laney snorted.

'It's hard for her, Elliott.'

Her mother's words were excruciatingly kind, but all they did was rile Laney up. 'Not you, too, Mum. I'm just *not interested*!'

'*Why* aren't you interested?' Elliott pushed, without really understanding why. It just felt really critical. 'When it's such a great opportunity?'

'I love it here. I don't want to leave. I don't want it to change.'

'It's all she knows,' Ellen piped up, her voice a study in compassion but her eyes closely focussed on her daughter.

And suddenly Elliott wondered if Ellen Morgan

was quite as sweet and passive as she seemed. Her words seemed very...calculated.

'I'm not afraid!' Laney insisted, reading very neatly between the lines.

'No, no. Of course not,' her mother gushed.

But the concept was hanging out there in public now, and—in a master stroke on her mother's part—it was Laney who'd put it there.

Her father spoke up again. 'I'm sure a country like the United States is very accommodating for people with vision impairment. And if they're not—'

Laney shot to her feet. 'It doesn't matter, because I'm not going to America.'

'I'll go,' Owen said, waving a lazy arm in the air as if he expected to be completely ignored. Which he pretty much was.

'We'll hire someone,' Robert went on.

Elliott tried not to be buoyed by his use of the future tense.

'Oh, please—you know me.' Laney sighed 'Do you think I'll be happy with the way anyone else does it? I'll end up doing it anyway.'

'Yeah, you will,' Elliott agreed. 'Because you can't help yourself, and because despite yourself you'll want this to be done well. Because that's the kind of person you are, Laney. A perfectionist.'

Owen snorted. 'That's one word for it.'

'Come on, Laney, you're intrigued. Admit it.'

'Because you *want* me to be, Elliott?'

'Because you *are*. I was watching you. You think the idea has merit. So do your parents.'

'Of course you'd say that.'

'Am I wrong?'

Her frown intensified and he knew he was right. She *was* interested.

'Carving the Morgan's logo into Mount Everest for PR has merit, too—doesn't mean we should do it.'

In his periphery, Robert and Ellen's glances ricocheted between him and their daughter like a tennis crowd.

'This is an outstanding opportunity for Morgan's. It will be a mistake not to take it.'

'No, what will be a mistake is to let our financier bully us into doing something that isn't on our radar.'

And by 'financier' she really meant him.

Elliott worked hard to keep his temper out of his voice. 'This is imploring, Laney, not bullying. This will *make* Morgan's. Just look at the figures.'

'Why do you even care? What is it to you? Other than your promotion.'

Good. At least she was prepared to acknowledge there was more at stake here than just his job. Not that she would have any idea of what was really at stake.

A man's soul.

'I hate to see this potential lost.'

'Life is full of disappointments, Elliott. You'll survive.'

She frowned as he crossed to stand right in front of her and took her hands in his. 'Laney. I know this is outside your comfort zone, but everyone in this room believes you can do it. You just have to believe in yourself. Be brave.'

The snatch as she pulled her hands back just about gave him whiplash.

'You assume this is about courage, Elliott. You call yourself a realiser, but what you really are is a *judger*.'

'I've been nothing but supportive of you.'

'You're judging me now. Finding me lacking because I don't want to take the risks you think I should. Well, people are built differently, Elliott, and it doesn't make them less. It just makes them different.'

'This could be massive for Morgan's.'

'Not everyone wants *massive*.'

'Why don't you? Why have you grown Morgan's this far only to stop. Why hold your family back?'

She reared up out of the chair. 'Everything I've

done I have done for my family. Don't you dare suggest otherwise.'

'They're not going to do this if you don't support it, Laney. You're the centre of this family. Everyone takes their cues from you.'

Her eyes sparkled magnificently. Dangerously. 'I guess that explains why you've put so much effort into winning *me* over, particularly.'

'Don't, Laney…'

'Why not? You win me over with your attention and your interest and your…your aftershave, and all of it was strategic. I'm the *Queen* of the Morgan's colony, after all.'

'This isn't about me, Laney—'

'This *is* about you, Elliott. You and your inability to accept anyone who isn't as driven as you.'

'Being driven is how people get things in life.'

'No, being driven is how *you* get things in *your* life. There're plenty of us who take a different route.'

He blew air between clenched teeth.

'Admit it, Elliott, you think I'm weak for not wanting this.'

'I don't think you're weak—'

'Despite all your flattering words, deep down you think I lack gumption. And you can't understand that in me any more than you could understand it in your mother. Admit it.'

Tension doubled deep inside. 'I do understand it in you, Laney. Your vision—'

'My vision has nothing to do with this. You're just using that as an excuse to justify it.'

'Justify what?'

'The fact I don't want to chase down every opportunity in life and kill it with a club. Well, guess what? It has nothing to do with my vision, Elliott, it's me—just me. My choice.'

'Laney—'

'And you know what? There are plenty of people just like me—just like your mother—who find their pleasures in simple ways. It doesn't make us faulty.'

Two forked lines appeared beneath Ellen Morgan's downturned eyebrows.

Elliott's gut clenched harder than his fists. 'This has nothing to do with my mother. This is about you letting your disability stop you from being everything you could be.'

The D-word hung out there, all ugly and un-retractable, in the sudden silence that followed.

'Why do I have to be everything?' she whispered harshly.

'Because you can. Because you shouldn't let anything get in your way.'

'Name me one thing that I could possibly have done that I've not tried in my life.'

There was one obvious answer.

'This,' Elliott said, low and hard. 'And I'd like to understand why.'

'Why...?' she squeaked. 'Maybe because I'm tired of being the poster child for the vision-impaired. I'm tired of the Morgan name coming up on Council minutes all through my childhood as Dad pushed for tactile strips on the main street or audiobook cassettes in the school library or modifications on the school bus to accommodate an assistance dog.'

Robert half croaked in protest and Laney snapped her face towards him.

'I'm sorry, Dad, I know you were trying to make life easier for me, but the world doesn't actually owe me anything. Maybe I didn't need to do every activity under the sun in order to be a full person. Or maybe I could have just found friends in my own time rather than you bussing them down and forcing us together just so we could all stay in denial about how different I was. Maybe it would have been okay for me to *not* try something out, or to just be ordinary at something, or—God forbid—even be bad at something. And maybe that's why I don't want to be railroaded into this. I *know*

I could do it but it should be enough for everyone that I *just don't want to.* I want to be here, on the property I love, working with the creatures I love and pursuing the things that interest *me.*'

She turned back to Elliott.

'Not my parents. Not Ashmore Coolidge. Not you.'

Silences didn't really come much thicker.

Laney shuffled in her seat but it did nothing to remove the discomfort of a hard truth finally aired.

'Honey,' her mother said finally, 'you never said.'

Laney flung her hands into the air. 'When is the right time to hurt your father? To throw your family's effort back in their face?'

Now, apparently.

'I love you both to death, but why isn't the person I am enough for anyone? Why do I always have to be…*more*?'

'Seriously, Laney?' Owen piped up. 'You're going to complain because you've had too many opportunities in life? When I'm sitting here trying to put my hand up for this one and the only person who *isn't* completely disregarding that is the person who barely knows me.'

She turned towards her brother. And she knew both her parents would be doing so too. 'You never put your hand up for things.'

'Why would I bother? Opportunities automatically go to you.'

'That's not true.'

'It's absolutely true, Laney. We were born at the same time but you got all the Royal Jelly in life. And you thrived. I turned out just a plain old worker.'

She sagged back into her chair.

'Why didn't you say?'

'Why didn't you ever tell Dad how you were feeling?'

Point taken.

What she wouldn't give right now to be able to look into her brother's eyes.

'You actually want to do this?' she whispered.

'I think I do.'

'But what about your surfing?'

'I love to surf, but I'm never going to be a pro. And fiddling with hives isn't enough for me. I'd like to do more. I *could* do more. And I'd really love to travel. There's a whole world out there, waiting to be seen.'

She snorted. 'You sound like Elliott.'

'I'll take that as a compliment. I think there's a lot I could learn from him. And you'd be a hypocrite to judge me for wanting to follow my own path.'

She soaked that in, then turned back towards Elliott. 'This wouldn't obligate us?'

'Phase one is fact-finding and relationship-building only. All decisions will come back here.'

'Could Owen do it?'

'With my help. I'll be there with him.'

Another excellent reason for her to say no. Travelling in close confines with Elliott and not being able to touch him? *Ugh,* imagine…

'How long would you be gone?' Robert asked, his voice still wounded.

'A couple of months. To get around to all the big suppliers personally and see the impact of winter on their spring.'

'Months? But we're going to need Owen to close out the season.'

'You mean *you* are,' Elliott said quietly. 'To be your eyes. And your driver. And your assistant.'

Her stomach rolled. Both at the ugliness of Elliott's statement and at its stark truth. He'd watched their operations closely enough to know exactly who did what. And for whom.

Oh, God…

Her chin sagged to her chest and mortification washed in around the realisation. She was as guilty of making presumptions about her brother's life as the world was about hers. Every time she brushed off an idea of his…every time she thought he was sweet for voicing an opinion. Owen didn't lack the grey matter to do more at Morgan's, he just wasn't engaged here. That was why he'd put his energies into other things, like surfing and girls. Because he'd trained himself not to care.

Because of her.

And he could learn a lot about business from Elliott. Things he'd probably never learn from his sister. Things that would give Owen the same kind of reward as the bees gave her.

The kind of reward he'd been forgoing all this time so that she could enjoy her life.

Tears stung dangerously at the back of her useless eyes.

'It's okay, Laney—' Owen started, genuinely aggrieved at her distress.

She shot a hand up to stop him. Because, no… It very definitely *wasn't* okay. Being blind was no excuse for what she'd failed to recognise. And she wasn't about to allow him to put himself second for her again.

A couple of months…

About the same time she'd known Elliott, and she'd managed to fall half in love with him in that time. Would a few months without him be enough to fall safely *out* of love again? At least she wouldn't have to deal with him every weekend.

She turned back towards her brother without consulting her parents. She knew them well enough to know what their silence meant.

She sighed.

'You're going to need a suit.'

'Are you okay?'

Elliott followed her outside when she took her leave from the awful family meeting. Awful, but probably necessary.

'I'm a horrible person.' She shuddered. No wonder Elliott didn't want her. Why would he?

His voice softened. 'No, you're not. Families are…complicated. Sometimes you have to step out of it to see it clearly.'

'I've hurt them all.'

'They'll live. Maybe today was just a day for saying overdue things.'

Mostly by her.

'I'm sorry if I set you up for that with my comments,' he murmured.

'It was the truth. And he wouldn't have his chance without your intervention.' Because she and her parents would still be dismissing Owen.

'What will you do while he's gone?' he asked.

'Hire someone in to help, maybe. Something we should have done years ago.'

'Why didn't you?'

Yeah…excellent question.

Her throat tightened. 'As long as Owen was a bit of a flunkie and helping me kept him positively occupied I got to hide behind the happy image of brother and sister working together. Contributing to the family together. And I got to overlook the hard truth.'

'Which was…?'

'That as long as it was my brother helping then I didn't have to feel disabled.'

'That's not the truth, Laney.'

'It's absolutely true. I let Owen believe that the only value he added to Morgan's was the one he brought to me. *I* did that, Elliott.' No wonder he was so desperate to stretch his wings. He was probably desperate for a bit of self-worth. 'I hadn't realised how self-absorbed I am.'

'You're not.'

'You said it yourself. I'm the Queen of my family.'

She heard the sag of his body in his voice. 'Laney…'

But, no… Being blind was no excuse for some of the things she'd been overlooking.

'It's a good proposal,' she admitted, desperate for a new subject. 'Congratulations.'

'This was never a contest.'

Wasn't it? From day one it had been a challenge to see who would outplay the other.

'You can still be involved,' he went on. 'As much as you want. Or as little.'

The latter was added with such reluctance. And shades of disdain. She lifted her head. 'Why are you pushing me so hard, Elliott?'

'Because you have so much more in you.'

More. Always *more*.

'What if I don't want to be more?'

What if she just wanted to be *her*.

'I don't believe that.'

'You mean you don't want to believe it.' She sighed. 'What happened to you to make you so intolerant of the choices of others?'

'Nothing happened. That's the point. Not one thing happened in my life unless I made it happen. Unless I went out and chased it down. Like you should.'

'I don't want to. I don't need to. I'm happy with my life exactly like it is.'

Well, mostly anyway. She wouldn't mind having a do-over with Owen. And a bit of love for a good man in the mix.

'I don't *need* to either, Laney.'

'Are you sure? Because it seems to me that someone who spends so much time sucking the guts out of life must have an awfully big space to fill inside. And all the cars and speedboats and penthouses and promotions and busyness will pad all that nothing out, but never really fill it.'

'You think I'm missing something?' he said, after the longest silence they'd ever shared.

Echoed in his voice it sounded more terrible than she'd meant it to. But why stop now with the revelations.

'Can I be honest?'

'Are you ever anything but?' he snorted.

'I think you have your priorities all messed up. I think you walked away from your only family because it was easier than addressing whatever it was going on inside you.'

'Based on the twenty seconds I've spent talking about my mother?'

'She made some hard choices, Elliott. She gave up her career to keep you and raise you.'

'She taught me to be afraid, Laney.'

'How?'

'Through example. She never encouraged me. She never believed in me. Just like you and your brother.'

The accusation stung. Because she could now see what her family's under-estimation had done to Owen's self-confidence. But the guilt only fired her up more.

'You beat your head against a brick wall trying to change her, and now you want to change me, too.'

'I don't want to change you.'

'You may not *want* to, Elliott, but I think you *have* to. Because me being happy and fulfilled exactly the way I am only highlights how empty you are.'

'Really? That's what you think?' His voice had chilled several degrees.

'I'm starting to.'

'And why exactly should it matter to me what you do? We're not a couple. We're barely even friends.'

A dull ache spread through her thorax. 'That's what I'd like to know. What is it to you?'

'I guess nothing,' he said, after an eternity, his voice rich with sorrow. 'I just wanted to help you.'

Poor little blind girl.

'I'm not your project, Elliott. I'm just asking you to respect my choices. To respect me.'

When he spoke again, his voice was hard. 'I don't think I can, Laney.'

Her gasp cracked the still air. She stared at him through her unseeing eyes. He couldn't bring himself to *respect* her?

'You're hiding out here in this paradise, Laney. A place and existence that's customised for you, that's as streamlined and predictable as the lives of your bees. And you've convinced yourself that you're happy that way because you don't know any different.'

'Any *better*, you mean?'

Could he be any more patronising?

A cold certainty washed over her. 'Is that why you stopped things between us last night? Because you can't be with someone you don't respect?'

His voice dropped. 'It's a pretty fundamental thing.'

Hurt clenched in her stomach. Yeah, it was. And pretty immutable, too.

She sagged back against the side of the house, struggling to breathe normally. All this time she'd just wanted to be accepted for who she was, but Elliott found it impossible to like that Laney.

Not much she could do about that.

'Well...' What the hell did you say in this situation? 'Good call, then. That would have been much more painful to discover if we'd got any more involved.'

You know—if I'd fallen in love with you or something...

She dropped her eyes in case he read the silent irony in them, unguarded. A silent minute ticked by.

'So, I guess I won't see you until I get back from

the trip,' he finally ventured, thick and low. 'I'll keep you informed—'

'No need. I'm sure Owen will be in touch regularly.'

Don't call me.

Despite his itchy feet, she felt sure that Owen would start missing his family about two minutes after leaving them. And, really, she'd get over Elliott much more quickly if he wasn't at the front of her consciousness, all glowing and present.

'Laney—'

She straightened and thrust out her hand. 'Goodbye, Elliott. I hope the trip is everything you want it to be.'

She stood there like that—hand outstretched, back straight, chin up—until his warm glove of a hand closed around hers. Firm. Tight.

A true goodbye shake.

And when he spoke his voice was no steadier than his hands.

'Bye, Laney. Take care.'

CHAPTER TWELVE

CRAWLING.

Just like the bees on the frames of the hives she checked multiple times each day, the weeks crawled by until they formed reluctant months.

Doing the hive runs wasn't as much fun with Rick as it was with her brother, but productivity sure was higher when Owen's replacement didn't pepper their every journey with side-trips and errands.

Maybe that had been Owen's way of making a dull job more interesting.

'Is this boring to you, Rick?' she asked between frames. About the job she adored.

'Nope. It's awesome.'

Thank you! 'Awesome because you've only been doing it a few weeks and the novelty hasn't yet worn off?'

'Awesome because it's outside.'

See? Rick got it. He'd scored a great job in a surf shop but then discovered he was basically a till jockey, trapped indoors all day, surrounded by boards and wetsuits and diving gear he could only use on the weekend. So he'd jumped at Owen's offer of filling in for him through autumn.

'And because I get to work with you,' he went on.

Laney fumbled the frame as she slid it back down and a heap of bees launched off with a slight angry-bee tone in their buzz.

Was that an overly appreciative *'work with you'*?

She'd always liked Rick, and considered him the better of her brother's friends, and they did have a lot in common, but there was no…*whatever*…with Rick. No spark. No intellectual attraction.

And definitely no glow.

The vacant place behind her eyes was still and dark when Rick was around. The light had been extinguished pretty much the day Elliott drove away from the farm for the last time.

'I'm sure I'm not that interesting.' She laughed carefully.

'Yeah, you are. I love watching you work with the bees. How they respond to you.' He closed one hive and moved to the next. 'But mostly I can just be myself around you, without worrying that you're working up to hitting on me.'

The hitch of anxiety in her chest that Rick was suggesting *more* fizzled into flat understanding. How like one of her brother's mates to be so utterly self-absorbed. And how contrary, on her part, that she should feel the stab of his rejection even when she didn't even want his interest. It really didn't help her to be reminded that the only man she'd welcome interest from was on the other side of the planet.

And found her philosophically repugnant.

As always, a deep ache took root low in her belly when she thought about Elliott and the way he'd judged her and found her wanting, and, as always, she forced it deeper, where she didn't have to think about it. Logically, she knew that she'd done her share of judging, too—echoes of the word *empty* came back to her at the most inconvenient moments—but as far as her heart was concerned the damage was all his.

'You should be so lucky,' she joked aloud.

They worked like that—casually chatting, but mostly getting on with the business of managing the hives—until their growling stomachs forced Rick back to the staff rest area for lunch and her back to the house to make a sandwich before her parents got back from the city with Owen in tow.

They'd cut their trip short because they'd had more business than any of them could have imagined fulfilling in their first year of exporting, leaving them all feeling very positive about the potential. But did her brother's enthusiastic reports

really need to come so liberally sprinkled with an-
ecdotes about Elliott?

Her brother's voice, but she *heard* Elliott.

Maybe it was just because he was the first person
to take Owen seriously. Or because he was so good
at what he did. So lateral and so driven. Maybe he
was just the first person to give Owen the right mix
of support, belief and education. To appreciate his
potential.

Now that Elliott had turned his full attention to
the *other* Morgan twin, ten weeks' intensive travel
had clearly birthed a serious bromance between the
two men.

And she could hardly blame Owen. She'd had one
herself for a while there.

Fortunately she'd had nearly three months of ab-
solute nothingness to wean herself off Elliott. Not
a word directly—only updates channelled through
her brother. That kind of total shut-down was as
good as a saturated blanket tossed on a grass fire.
Total spark-killer. Even the glow had retreated to
something that only emerged when she let herself
think about him in any way outside of the strictly
professional.

Which was never.

So everything she knew about what he'd been up
to she heard from her brother or her parents. And

once from when she web-searched Elliott in a moment of lapsed self-discipline.

She settled in at her desk with her sandwich—at the computer that had freaked Elliott out so much because it didn't have a monitor—and checked her email for something from Owen. Although of course there'd be nothing from Owen, because he would have been in the air for the past twenty-four hours.

So really this was about Elliott.

Of course it was. It was his name she was secretly hoping to hear her text-reader announce. But, no. Nothing.

She keyed the software to instant sleep and reached for the phone instead.

Time for this to end.

'Welcome to Ashmore Coolidge,' an *über*-professional voice answered.

'Helena Morgan for Elliott Garvey, please.'

The faultless voice stumbled. 'Uh…one moment please.'

It hit her then, blazing and obvious—maybe he'd taken the day off since his international flight had only landed this morning. Assuming he'd flown back with Owen at all. And right after that she realised that she didn't know his home number. Or his address. Ashmore Coolidge was her one and only channel to Elliott.

'This is Roger Coolidge, Ms Morgan.'

Senior partner Roger Coolidge? Surely Elliott didn't get to bump his work *up* the food chain while he was away on business?

She stiffened. 'Mr Coolidge, I'm so sorry to have troubled you—'

'How can I help you, Ms Morgan?'

Time is money. Right. 'I was calling for Elliott. I've just realised he's probably not back in the office until tomorrow.'

'Elliott?' he repeated, as though her use of his Christian name was somehow inappropriate. 'Garvey?'

'I have…um…some questions about the Morgan's proposal.' Total rubbish, but somehow she couldn't imagine Roger Coolidge responding positively to *I just want to hear his voice.*

'The export proposal?'

How many proposals were there? 'I just wanted to see how it was tracking.'

Ugh, such a bad liar.

Office sounds clanked away in the background of Roger Coolidge's silence. 'Ms Morgan, Elliott Garvey is no longer employed at Ashmore Coolidge. I assumed you'd been informed.'

Her stomach dropped away, along with her only lifeline to Elliott. 'What? No...'

'As of several months ago.'

But their proposal... 'Why?'

His voice grew softer. Kinder. 'I'm not really at liberty to say—'

'Elliott Garvey is in possession of a lot of our financial data,' she improvised—badly. 'I would have thought as our financial advisors you would recognise the necessity of my question.'

The kindness evaporated. Utterly. She should have known better than to try and play someone as experienced as Roger Coolidge.

'Ms Morgan... He left of his own accord after we rejected his proposal for Morgan's.'

Rejected?

'He left?' The job and the company he loved? His promotion fast-track? 'Why?'

'We disagreed on some of the...conditions of approval. He was inflexible and opted to leave when we denied the proposal.'

'What conditions?'

'Again, I'm not at liberty to say. You'll need to ask him.'

'How, if he's not our rep any more?'

'My understanding is that he's with one of your

personnel in the United States right now, pursuing the proposal privately.'

Those last words were strained.

'Well, I—'

'If you have any questions relating to Ashmore Coolidge's services, or its current work with Morgan's, I'd be happy to have Garvey's replacement contact you personally...'

The rest was a blur of impatient political correctness until Roger Coolidge disentangled them both from the awkwardness of the conversation and hung up.

Laney squeezed the phone hard in her hand.

Gone.

Proposal rejected. Promotion jettisoned.

Yet Elliott hadn't told them before whisking Owen off overseas. What had he done after his proposal was rejected? Taken his bat and ball and decided to play on by himself? To go for the money if he couldn't have the promotion? Show them what a mistake they'd made?

Was he that desperate to succeed? Or was it just ego, frustration and maybe even anger at the lack of vision shown by his superiors—men he was supposed to respect?

Though she knew what a big deal respect was to him.

Unfortunately.

But more pressing… Ashmore Coolidge was the only way she knew of getting in touch with Elliott now that he was back from his travels. And there was something terrifyingly final about not having one single communication channel to someone you loved…

'Knock-knock.'

Rick's deep voice sounded just inside the front door and sent her leaping out of her chair and Wilbur scrabbling to his feet, both of them as guiltily as if he'd caught them up to no good.

'There's a dust plume coming in from the highway,' he announced.

Owen.

It occurred to her suddenly to wonder if he'd have Elliott with him and her heart began thumping in earnest.

'One plume or two?'

And she held her breath.

'Just the one.' He kept on talking over her plunging hopes until he finished up with, 'Is that okay with you?'

'Um…sure.' Whatever she'd just agreed to. If her vacant expression didn't give her away.

'Great. I'll see you tomorrow, then. Say hi to Owen for me.'

And then he was gone, leaving her with just enough time to finish her sandwich and brush the pollen out of her hair, thoroughly distracted, before the return of the prodigal son.

'Lake Erie.'

Her mother had given up describing what was in the photos at image number eighty-seven. Now Laney was lucky if each picture in Owen's excited slideshow even got a descriptor name.

Part of her would have liked to '*see*' Lake Erie. But another part of her—the part that really would have preferred to be doing something more productive with these hours—figured she could pull up a few pictures on the internet and have her mother describe those instead. At a more mutually enjoyable time.

A time when her thoughts weren't so completely filled with thoughts of a different man.

She'd made a total fool of herself, nervously holding her breath as first Owen, then her mother and finally her father had alighted from her dad's wagon. A pathetic part of her had desperately wanted to hear a fourth door-slam.

But there had been no fourth slam.

Owen in full so-tired-he-was-wired mode after his epic flight from the US was just a babbling sequence of stories with barely a breath drawn between them. And every story featured Elliott one way or another.

Elliott did this... Elliott said that... Here's Elliott at the biggest apiary in the States...

Ugh.

'I need to go for a walk.' She cut across her brother's slideshow narration, surprising herself with the intention and pushing to her feet.

'Right now?' her father asked. 'But your brother's only just back.'

She pushed to her feet and felt for her coat before there could be any dissent. Apparently, yes, right now. 'I need some air.'

And she needed—very badly—to extract herself from the Elliott Garvey show.

She felt her way to where Owen sat and kissed the top of his head. His gorgeous surf locks were gone in favour of a much more business-like short haircut. Somehow that made him even more a whole new Owen.

'Good to have you back, O.'

'We need to talk later,' he threatened—and that was really the only word for the sudden seriousness in his voice. Owen—the man who was never serious about anything.

Wilbur groaned as he heaved himself to his feet,

and she surprised herself again by signalling him to stay. He sank his old bones back down gratefully. 'I won't go far,' she assured him.

But she was lying, and his slight doggie whine told her he knew it.

Staying close was safe, and safe wasn't what she burned for just now. *Safe* was what Elliott had accused her of being all those weeks ago. Something deep inside her wanted to prove him wrong. Wanted to show him—or maybe just herself—that she could take as many risks as the next person.

As *him*.

She grabbed up her stick as she left the house and all Owen's exciting stories behind and turned left towards the coast track.

What she wouldn't have given for a bigger butt right now.

Laney shifted from one cheek to the other on the rocky track and flexed tired, sore muscles, then tipped her face up to the sun to give her flagging spirits a boost.

Stupid.

She had her phone, but she wasn't about to use it to call for help. In fact she'd turned it off so that no one could ring her, either, and offer to help. That would defeat the entire purpose of her ridiculous trek up to the lookout without Wilbur. The furthest point she could imagine going on foot. Somewhere she'd never been alone before.

Somewhere not entirely safe.

The lookout was a statement, and that statement was not going to be strengthened by a call for the cavalry to rescue her from the stupid stone she'd twisted her ankle on.

But two hours on her butt in the dust and her throbbing joint wasn't easing off any. She'd enjoyed the first hour—had used it to think and to gently test her abused ankle, to stretch out the yank on her tendons, waiting for the *ouch* to ease. But two hours without any improvement and she was starting to question the wisdom of this whole impetuous statement.

All she'd done was prove Elliott right, really.

Still she didn't use her phone. She'd spend the night out here before calling for help. Turned ankles were hardly a new experience for her—she just needed to wait it out. Although she would turn for home just as soon as her leg was up to the challenge. There really was no point in denying reality.

She was *blind*.

And this was *far*.

She tipped her face back and stared straight into the sun, her ears full of the wind buffeting the coast, her perception full of the golden glow of the sun. And she used it to calm her anxious nerves.

'Hey...'

Her ankle protested at her startled lurch. And the sun's glow turned rich and masculine.

Elliott...

'Whatcha doing, Laney?'

'Thinking,' she replied, struggling not to move. Struggling for some dignity. Struggling not to weep at the sound of his voice.

'On the ground?'

'Benches seem to be in short supply out here.'

'Yeah, you're a long way from home,' he murmured, squatting next to her.

'I could say the same thing.'

Why are you here? That was what she wanted to say. And right behind that was an immense gratitude that he was.

'Your phone is off.'

Heat washed up her neck but she lifted her chin anyway. 'I prefer to do my thinking in silence.'

'Are you planning on getting up any time soon?'

'When I'm ready.'

But this man was no fool. His sharp brain was one of the things she loved best about him. The present tense of that thought sucked at her spirits. All her good work of the past two months undone by mere moments back in Elliott's company.

Her feelings for him hadn't changed one little bit.

'Laney, are you hurt?'

Horribly! she wanted to sob. By everything he'd shown her about herself. And about himself. And about the unfairness of life in general.

She waved her left leg loosely. 'My ankle.'

His answer was immediate and infuriating. But she was too distracted by the heaven of his arms around her after all this time, and by his scent pressing so close to her, to protest as he lifted her off the ground. He resettled her more comfortably and her arms crept around his neck.

Where she'd once let herself believe they belonged.

'What are you doing here?' she asked, breathless, as his footfalls crunched.

'Looking for you.'

Ugh…such intensity. How badly did she want to imagine that it had something to do with her and was not because her parents had issued some kind of all-points bulletin?

'Lower your good foot.'

She slid down his body, with the polished gloss of his car at her back, until her strong foot hit the ground. He opened the door with one hand and helped her inside with the other.

'I mean on the peninsula,' she said as soon as he'd closed himself in with her. 'Why are you here?'

Looking for you. Please say it…please say it.

But his voice was guarded. 'I've spent the last ten weeks on the go in the constant company of your brother. My apartment felt pretty big and echoey all of a sudden.'

'And you thought you'd remedy that by driving four hundred kilometres to hang out on one of our windswept cliffs?'

She refused to let his chuckle warm her.

'I thought you'd have gone to the office if you were in need of company,' she tested. 'I'm sure it's full of people working way past their home time.'

'I stopped off to see my mother, but otherwise I headed straight down from the airport.'

Nice hedge. She straightened further as he by-passed confession, but played along. 'How is she?'

'She's good. She—' He stopped as suddenly as if something had caught his eye in the distance. 'We had a good chat.'

What? Could he barely believe his own words?

'About your trip?'

'About a whole bunch of things. Overdue things. Turns out I had my share of unspoken baggage there.'

'You shock me.'

He didn't take offence.

'Did you get it sorted?'

Because mothers mattered.

'Yeah. I think we did. There was a lot I didn't understand.'

'Like what?'

'Like how I came about.'

'Elliott, I could have given you the birds and the bees talk if I'd realised you were lacking…'

'Funny girl. I mean *why*. Turns out Mum was acting out when she was sixteen. Trying to get herself fired from the squad.'

'Why?'

'She was miserable. She hated that life. She hated the pressure she'd been put under her whole childhood. The stress. The intense expectation.'

'So getting pregnant was her solution?'

'Getting pregnant was just the result. She knew fraternisation would get her sent home.'

'So you *made* her life, then? Not ruined it?' His earlier words echoed, clear and pained.

'I changed it. But…' A gentle lightness stole over

his deep voice. 'Yeah, not for the worse, as far as she was concerned.'

It was hard to resent a man for his own personal healing. Even one who had hurt you.

'I'm glad for you. Does that help?'

'It explains a lot. Her background too. Now I know why she didn't push me harder. Or at all. She thought she was protecting me from the sort of experience she'd had. Letting me just emerge at my own pace.'

'But you wanted the pressure?'

'I wanted her belief.'

Yeah. Laney could definitely relate to that.

'Let me just call your parents,' he said. 'They are frantic. And Owen's cursing because you've up-staged his glorious return.'

No. Not the Owen who had come back from his travels. That Owen was infinitely more self-assured than the one who had left. But she sighed anyway. 'It seems I haven't really learned anything in the months you were gone.'

Except that wasn't true. She'd learned how to be humble. And that a person couldn't just *wish* feelings away. More was the pity.

'Where were you headed?' he asked after a brief call to her brother. 'Before gravity intruded?'

'The lookout.'

'You weren't far off. I can see it from here. Why so far from home?'

'I can't really explain it… I needed to do it. To prove I could.' Never mind that apparently she couldn't. She shuddered in a calming breath. 'I hate that you were right.'

He could have said something comforting, something patronising. But he didn't. He shifted in his seat, turning his voice more fully on her. 'You want to tell me what's really going on, Laney?'

'I could ask you the same,' she murmured.

'What do you mean?'

Enough of the eggshells, already. 'You lied to us.'

His surprise was more of a stammer. 'About what?'

'About not representing Ashmore Coolidge any longer. About quitting your job in protest when they denied the export proposal.'

Awkward.

'I didn't lie, Laney.'

'Yeah, you did.'

'No, I didn't. I emailed your father with full details when it happened. Did he not tell you?'

She thought back to how injured her father had been after that evening, and how long it had taken the two of them to get back to a cautious happy place where he finally understood the pressure he'd put on his young daughter, with his relentless drive to give her every experience available, and she'd finally accepted that those same experiences had nurtured and drawn out her talents. Made her the woman she now was.

'Guess he forgot.'

Unless he was just too hurt…

'Or he didn't want you to worry about Owen.'

'Why would I worry about Owen?'

'Because there's a big difference between heading Stateside under the auspices of an international finance company and two freelancers cold-calling in a rented RV.'

'There may be things about my brother that I was unaware of, Elliott, but I know Owen well enough to recognise that the latter would have suited him down to the ground.'

'He did really well.'

The proud confirmation of a mentor. And a friend.

'So…what happened with Ashmore Coolidge? Why did you leave?'

'Water under the bridge, Laney. Wouldn't you rather talk about the trip?'

Actually, what she wanted to say was *Why didn't you call me?* But his ex-employers seemed a much safer topic. And one likely to keep him at a distance.

'No. I want to talk about Ashmore Coolidge.'

'They passed on the deal. Ripples from the global financial crisis.'

'You don't seem the type to poach a client.'

'I'm not. I told them when I resigned that I was going to pursue it with your family. Independently.'

'And they were okay with that?' Not the Roger Coolidge she'd spoken to.

'They didn't love it, but they were prepared to be flexible after...'

'After what?'

'Laney, it really doesn't matter.'

'It does to me. If there are good reasons why we shouldn't be proceeding.'

'They aren't related to the feasibility or the figures. And they aren't good reasons.'

'Then what?'

'Look, Laney. I believed in the proposal and I believe in Morgan's. And I really believed in the opportunity. Too much to just let it go.'

'What about your promotion?'

'I walked away.'

For a guy whose dream had been ripped out from under him he sounded pretty...relaxed. 'I want to say I'm sorry about that, but something tells me I shouldn't.'

'I can't say I enjoyed the face-down with my em-

ployers, but a couple of months of being freelance
has shown me how much I've been missing by teth-
ering myself to a company as conservative as Ashmore Coolidge.'

'Face-down about what?'

Frustration issued tight and tense from his throat.
'A fundamental aspect of their approval.'

Wait. There'd been a moment when they *would*
have accepted? And he hadn't jumped at it? 'Come
on, Elliott, you know I'm not going to stop asking.'

'Laney, can you just trust me that I did what I
thought was in your best interests?'

'"*Your best interests*" Morgan's—or "*Your best
interests*" mine?'

'Laney—'

She reached for her phone. 'Maybe I'll just ask
Roger, then.'

Strong fingers curled around hers to stop her di-
alling. '*Roger?* You're on a first-name basis with
Coolidge?'

'A lot has changed since you've been gone.'

*You know—in the time when you were completely
ignoring me.*

'I'm amazed he wasn't too ashamed…' he said,
under his breath.

'Of what, Elliott?'

Breath hissed out of him like a deflating balloon.

'Ashmore Coolidge made acceptance of my proposal only on certain conditions—' That was the world Roger Coolidge had used, too. '—and certain marketing strategies that I didn't agree with.'

'Carving our logo into Mount Everest?'

'Actually, I thought that had merit,' he quipped.

But his silence only grew more awkward, and she recognised that awkwardness from those first hours when they'd met. 'Wait... Was it to do with me?'

Silence.

'What did they want you to do?'

'You weren't even comfortable with the researchers naming their project after you. I was pretty sure you wouldn't have wanted to be the international face of Morgan's.'

Correct.

'Ashmore Coolidge particularly wanted *your* face,' he nudged.

'Did they imagine a pretty face would open doors with the apiaries?'

His sigh was almost lost in the rasp as he ran his hands over his chin. 'They felt you would open doors on the media circuit.'

And then the penny finally dropped. And rolled right off the edge of the cliff behind them. 'They wanted to trade off my vision?'

'It's not going to happen, Laney.'

'Damn right, it's not! I can't believe they asked.'

'They don't know you.'

'Do they not have any shame?' Heck, and she'd been so polite to Roger Coolidge!

'If they did they'd never do half the things they do.'

But as her umbrage eased off a little the meaning of his words sank in. She twisted back towards him and whispered, 'You quit your job rather than sell me out?'

'I found a line I wouldn't cross. Who knew?'

His laugh was one hundred per cent self-deprecation.

No. He was making light of it, but just...*no*. 'You gave up your dream.'

For *me*.

'It was repugnant, Laney.'

So...what...? Anyone would have done it? Did he expect her to believe that?

'Not to them. They would have quite happily used my blindness to sell a truckload of honey.'

'Don't deify me just yet, Laney. I walked away from that opportunity straight into another one. A better one. I wasn't exactly taking a leap of faith. If we proceed, I stand to make that same truckload.'

'So you're in this for you? You're not a good guy? That's what you want me to believe?'

'I'm a reasonable guy, Laney, but I'm not a saint. There was a time your vision was on the assets side of *my* assessment file. Back at the start.'

Sure, he'd thought about it—but he hadn't done it. Big difference.

'What stopped you?'

'You. I got to know you.'

Her heart clenched before she remembered not to let it. 'I don't need you to run interference for me with Ashmore Coolidge. I would have told them where they could shove that idea.'

His full laugh washed over her like a warm wave. It had been a long time since she'd heard it.

'I know. It wasn't about you. It was about me. Drawing that line.' He cleared his throat. 'I didn't want to be a man who had no line.'

A decency line. And she was it. But not because of *her*; because of him.

'Thank you,' she murmured. 'For whatever reason you did it. You had a lot to lose.'

'I have a lot to gain, too.' He took her hands in his again. 'Laney, it took me a while, but I got there. I understand you don't want to be defined by your vision. The woman who does extraordinary things *despite* her blindness. Or *because* of it. You don't even want to be extraordinary.'

'Wasted potential, I'm sure you'd say.'

'Yeah, I would have—before I met you. Because before then…you were right…I associated potential with achievements. Things. Value. I had no idea that the most important potential is the person that we are.' Breath sighed out of him. 'And you're the most fully realised person that I've ever met, Helena Morgan.'

She swallowed, but couldn't think of one clever thing to say.

'It took me a few weeks away from you to see it clearly. And lots of conversations with your brother—who worships the ground you walk on, by the way. I'm the one that's been dipping out on my potential. In favour of money and status. Glossing over relationships, skipping from country to country, never settling in one place long enough that it became obvious. But I can't stand next to you for more than a few minutes before I start to feel inadequate.'

'You're hardly that.'

Confusion leached out of him. 'I'm not happy. Not like you are. I'm not content in my own company and with my life the way I've built it. I'm rich, and I'm well-travelled, but I don't get up each morning and just…smile.'

'You say that like you have no experience of happiness at all.'

'My mother chose her simple life as an antidote to the first sixteen years of her life. All that pressure. All that expectation from her parents and her coaches since she was five years old. She was happy—genuinely happy—and healing through our simple life. But I couldn't be. I was ambitious and proud, even as a kid, and the absence of her encouragement and support really rankled. I hated myself for finding my own mother so lacking, but that was easier than looking at what was really going on. She had nothing in life yet she seemed so full. And I had nothing in life but was also completely dissatisfied. Completely empty. All that travel, all that accumulation, was to compensate for the great nothing I felt inside.'

'I was angry when I said you were empty—'

'You were *right* when you said it.' He turned her towards him. 'Turns out I'm the real blind one here, and I've been fumbling around in the dark for years, in that same emotional metre-square, avoiding real relationships, avoiding giving myself to anything, thinking that's all there is. And then I met you, and you showed me this whole other world I was missing.' His fingers threaded through hers. 'But I didn't hold on hard enough. You were my guide and I let you go.'

Everything in her shrivelled into an aching ball.

Was he saying she was his Wilbur? When he knew full well that Wilbur meant everything to her.

'A whole other world?' she croaked.

'I just wanted to return the favour, Laney. I didn't know that was what I was doing in trying to get you off the farm, but I was trying to give you *my* world.'

'I thought you pitied me.'

'I know.'

'I thought my lack of ambition repelled you.'

His hand tightened around hers. 'I'm so sorry that's how I made you feel.'

'You made me feel impaired. And I'd truly never felt that until then. In all my life.'

The silence then was awful. But she took some solace from the fact that he at least recognised that to have been the cruellest thing he could do to her. So maybe he did know her a little bit, after all.

His forehead leaned gently on hers, and it was more eloquent than anything he could have said just then.

'I have nothing against new things,' she murmured into the silence. 'Or places. I just object to being expected to do them or go to them because I somehow *owe* it to blind people everywhere. I was even a little bit jealous that Owen was off having this great time—*with you*—and having experiences I might never get to have. But the more everyone expected me to do it the less I wanted to. On principle.'

'You don't need to explain. And I don't ever want you putting yourself at risk like today just to show me you can.'

'I think I needed to show *me* I could,' she admitted. 'And so when I couldn't it was confronting'

He drew her into a careful embrace—welcoming, not forcing. So that she could disentangle herself if she wanted. But she didn't want. She'd been missing these arms for months.

'You're not empty, Elliott,' she breathed.

'Not when we're together,' he vowed. 'Empty doesn't feel like this.'

Their combined body heat warmed his scent and it shimmied around them. She nestled more fully into his hold and was warmed through from the inside out.

'Bees do this,' she murmured against his chest. 'The "cuddle death". The workers embrace the retiring Queen, *en masse*, until the combined heat of their vibrating wings means she gently expires.'

And right now, in the warmth of Elliott's hold, she'd have happily ended her days just like this.

'Nice analogy.' He leaned away from her slightly, to murmur against her hair. 'If a little creepy.'

Maybe it was because this was the first time she'd

really laughed in months. Or maybe it was because a matching one rattled through his big body and vibrated against her cheek. But whatever the reason it gave her the confidence to be truly vulnerable with him.

'I missed you so much, Elliott.'

'Ditto.'

And then they were kissing again. After such a long hiatus. His finger under her chin lifted her waiting mouth for the press of his warm lips, the challenge of his tongue, and the comfort of his hot breath mingling with hers. And somehow she knew that he was the last man she would ever kiss.

No matter what happened from here.

He broke away from her gently to start the car and reversed, only to park again.

'What are we doing?' she murmured, twisting back towards him.

'I wanted to look at the view. Morgan's is spread out in front of me.'

'You haven't been gone that long, Elliott. It hasn't changed.'

'I want you to understand that I know exactly what I'm taking on by loving you. The whole Morgan package.'

Her heart plunged to her stomach and then did its best to beat there, awkwardly wedged below her diaphragm. Her breath grew laboured. Excruciatingly so.

Loving you?

'America was agony, Laney, despite your brother's best attempts at being good company. I should have been ecstatic—we were slaying the opposition and signing memoranda of understanding everywhere we went—but the only time my spirits lifted above sea level was when Owen spoke about you. Or gave me news about you from home. Eventually it got so bad he'd intentionally hold back snippets to give me just before we walked into an appointment. So I'd be on my game.'

'We need to talk...' her brother had vowed when she'd left home earlier today. She'd thought he meant about their own relationship, but maybe he was wanting to tell her about Elliott.

Loving you.

But years of protection were hard to walk away from. 'What are you saying?'

'I'm saying I understand what I'm accepting by loving you. All of that land. All of that heritage. I understand what I'm giving up, too, and I want you to believe that I'm ready to do it. I have nothing of value in the city. Everything I need is right here on this lookout.'

Elation threatened to lift her two feet above his

plush leather seats. But still she couldn't trust it. 'What about parasailing?'

Big hands framed her face, stroked the ridges of her cheekbones. 'Hmm, good point. Okay, you and parasailing are the only things that I love. Conveniently, both of which I can have on the peninsula.'

'You'll go mad sitting on the farm,' she breathed, and it was far more wobbly than she preferred. 'Like Owen.'

'I wouldn't have to sit. I could be like one of your worker bees, flying out, strengthening the business, then returning to the property.' He brushed a lock of hair back from her face. 'Returning to my Queen.'

Well... Could she trust this to be real? 'With a stomach full of nectar?'

'And pollen balls wadded up under my armpits.'

A smile broke through entirely without her permission and she realised that, yes, she could trust this moment. More importantly, she could trust this man.

She wriggled more comfortably into his arms. 'You think you can just swan in and exploit all our hard work to make an easy fortune?'

'You think life with you is going to be easy? Pfff...' He kissed her, fast and hard. 'Besides, I'm not swanning in. I'm buying in. At great expense. I want to be a Morgan's partner, regardless.'

'Regardless of what?'

'Of whether you love me back or not.'

She kept her lashes low in case her traitorous eyes broadcast her thoughts. 'You doubt my feelings?'

'I don't know what to think. You're protecting yourself.'

'Does that surprise you?'

'No, I definitely get it. But I'm not taking anything for granted. Even if it's all too soon between us now, we have years of working together—as partners—to get to know each other fully. Maybe I can make some headway on winning you over.'

As if that ship hadn't sailed weeks ago.

'How?'

'By loving you. And believing in you. And returning to you on the trade winds like the good drone that I am.'

She found his mouth with her fingers and then kissed him long and hard. When she was done she spoke against his lips. 'If you're a drone, that means we only get one night together. And that's not going to be nearly enough.'

'If that's all I get, I'll take it.'

'And what if I want you to have more?'

His arms circled more tightly around her and his thighs pressed flat against hers. 'Then I'm yours. However much—or little—you want.'

'You think I might not want more?'

'I just don't want to make any assumptions.'

No. Because she hadn't given him any reason not to yet. Time for that to change.

'I love you, Elliott. As fast and crazy as that seems. You are the most important person in my life.'

Laney's senses reeled as he plunged his fingers into her hair and his lips half devoured hers.

But then the spinning slowed and he pulled slightly away. 'Wait a minute—do you mean the most important *non-hairy* person in your world?'

Wilbur. 'Is that going to be a problem?'

'Whatever it takes. Just so long as you will always be my Queen.'

EPILOGUE

Four years later

THE HIGH-PITCHED SQUEALS and delirious barking merged together into one of Laney's most favourite sounds as she sat, her hand resting gently on a curve of stones, atop her favourite hill, occasionally visited by bees from her favourite hive.

Best sound ever.

A girl and her dog.

Running and playing and just loving each other so intensely. Even though he wasn't technically her dog to love. Even though he had a serious job to do.

Those kinds of distinctions were meaningless when you were three years old.

All little Ashleigh Morgan Garvey cared about was that her three great loves loved her back: *Mummy,* who gave her the best cuddle death hugs of all time, *Daddy,* who let her sneak into bed with them for three nights straight after every plane trip away, and her *'woof buddy',* who was the most grown-up three-year-old Ashleigh had ever met.

Born the same year as Ashleigh and delivered fully assistance-trained—and festooned in a bow on the day of the ceremony they'd very belatedly got around to organising—Toby had been a wedding gift from her husband, who'd recognised what she'd been unable to admit.

The future.

Laney sipped at the cup of tea in her right hand and patted the stones by her thigh as she so often did. And—as it so often did—it brought her peace and comfort and an incredible feeling of rightness with the world.

Her beautiful husband—who was away as much as Morgan's needed but at home every other waking minute—had helped her collect every rock. He'd made the jarrah cross and then helped her engrave the letters with her own hands—not perfectly level, not even properly punctuated, but every letter packed with love and devotion. And he'd held her tight and patient in his arms as she'd cried her heart out at the loss of the first great love of her life.

Wilbur. 'Toby!'

A split-second warning before fifteen kilograms of puppy-at-heart splashed warm tea all over her hand. And then he was off again. Being a regular dog, because his harness was off. She rested her mug on the ground.

'Hello, Wilbur,' Ashleigh whispered to the stones, slumping down into her mother's lap and tucking her little arms around her.

They sat there like that for priceless, precious moments, and a glow more blazing and complete than any other she'd known filled her consciousness.

'Daddy's coming,' Ashleigh said in hot little breaths under her jaw, as much a scene-setter as her grandmother. 'He's got some papers.'

'Thank you.'

'I love Daddy.'

Laney smiled and rubbed her left thumb on her daughter's cheek. 'Me, too, chicken.'

'What am I missing?' Elliott's deep, sexy voice rumbled as he bent and plucked his daughter from her lap.

Laney leaned back into the strength of his long legs the same way she leaned back into his arms—his chest—in front of the fire in their timber house up near the lookout.

'Just two girls chatting about the men they love.'

'Girl-talk, huh? I guess I should get used to it. I've got a lifetime of it ahead.'

Laney put one hand on her belly and the other brushed again over the smooth stones on Wilbur's grave. Both touches as comforting as each other. 'You never know. This one might be a boy.'

'Not a chance.' Elliott's honey voice rained down on her. 'Our little colony is going to be as female-dominated as a hive. I can feel it.'

'Would you mind?'

'Nope. Not if they're all as clever and strong as you.'

'And if they're not?'

'Then they'll be unique in some other way. And I'll love them just as much. No matter what.'

No matter what.

No expectations, no conditions, no pressure. Just love and support. Just as it should be.

She leaned back into him and let the glow surge, growing and engulfing everyone and everything around them. Elliott, Ashleigh and her unborn sibling, and Wilbur's final resting place. The emotional brightness brought moisture to her sightless eyes, but it was a good kind of damp—the best kind—and she decided that, if nothing else, *that's* what her eyes were good for.

For loving her family.

* * * * *